T5-DHV-801

GOLDEN DRAGON
FANTASY GAMEBOOKS

You are a skilled adventurer who has roamed far
and wide, always ready to hire your sword for a fistful
of gold. In your yearning for constant challenge and
the excitement of battle you have fought trolls, orcs,
goblins, mad warlocks and many other strange and
terrifying opponents. And you have always won. The
years of adventure have honed your reflexes and fighting skill so that few men could hope to stand against
you in single combat.

But be warned: this adventure is not easy. You are
highly unlikely to defeat the evil demon Slank on your
first attempt. It may take several attempts, but eventually you will win through to engage the arch-fiend
in combat and release the tormented souls he has
imprisoned.

And now—the adventure begins…

GOLDEN DRAGON
FANTASY GAMEBOOKS
6

CASTLE OF LOST SOULS

DAVE MORRIS & YVE NEWNHAM
Illustrated by Leo Hartas

 BOOKS FOR YOUNG ADULTS

B

BERKLEY BOOKS, NEW YORK

A different and shorter version of this adventure appeared in
White Dwarf magazine in May-July 1984.

This Berkley/Pacer book contains the complete
text of the original edition.

CASTLE OF LOST SOULS

A Berkley/Pacer Book, published by arrangement with
Grafton Books

PRINTING HISTORY
Dragon Books edition published 1985
Berkley/Pacer edition / December 1986

ISBN: 0-425-09417-0

Pacer is a trademark belonging to
The Putnam Publishing Group.

A BERKLEY BOOK ® TM 757,375
Berkley/Pacer Books are published by The Berkley Publishing Group,
200 Madison Avenue, New York, NY 10016.
The name "BERKLEY" and the "B" logo are
trademarks belonging to Berkley Publishing Corporation.

PRINTED IN THE UNITED STATES OF AMERICA

10 9 8 7 6 5 4 3 2

To Jamie

CASTLE OF LOST SOULS

INTRODUCTION

Imagine how it would feel to be Indiana Jones, or Conan the Barbarian, or Luke Skywalker. Rather than merely sitting back and watching somebody else's adventures, the thrill and danger would be yours to experience at first hand. Only your own skill and daring, and the decisions you made, would stand between you and a hundred hideous deaths.

In the Golden Dragon Gamebooks, you *are* the hero.

You are a skilled adventurer who has roamed far and wide, always ready to hire your sword for a fistful of gold. In your yearning for constant challenge and the excitement of battle you have fought trolls, orcs, goblins, mad warlocks and many other strange and terrifying opponents. And you have always won. The years of adventure have honed your reflexes and fighting skill so that few men could hope to stand against you in single combat.

To determine just how good an adventurer you are, you must use the dice:

Roll two dice. Add 20 to this number and enter the total in the VIGOUR box on your Character Sheet. This score represents your strength, fitness and general will to survive. Any wounds you take during your quest are subtracted from your VIGOUR score. If it ever reaches zero you are dead.

Roll one die. Add 3 to the number rolled and enter the total in the PSI box on your Character Sheet. The higher this score, the better you are at resisting spells cast at you and the more sensitive you are to psychic impressions.

Roll one die, add 3 and enter the total in the AGILITY box. This score reflects how nimble you are. You will need a high AGIITY to scale walls, leap across chasms, and so on.

YOUR NAME

Personalize your adventuring persona by thinking of a heroic name. You might call yourself Lucas Starkiller or Sir Bergan the Bold, Lady Angela Centuri or Li Chun the Black Dragon, or any other name you can think of. Imagine what sort of adventurer you are first – a noble knight, a crafty rogue, a dashing swordsman or a rugged Viking, perhaps – and then choose a name to reflect your personality.

VIGOUR, AGILITY and PSI

Your VIGOUR will change constantly during the adventure – every time you are wounded, in fact. You may acquire healing potions or salves on your quest. These will restore some of the VIGOUR points you have lost owing to wounds – but unless you are told otherwise your VIGOUR score must never exceed its original value. This is your *normal* score, and you must keep a careful note of it.

Your AGILITY and PSI are less likely to change, although this is possible. Spraining your ankle, for example, might reduce your AGILITY by 1 point. A magic helmet might increase your PSI. But, as with VIGOUR, your AGILITY and PSI will never exceed their *normal* scores unless you are specifically told otherwise.

You can keep your scores on this Character Sheet, in pencil so that they can be rubbed out for further adventures, or you may wish to copy it out each time.

CHARACTER SHEET

VIGOUR Current score: 32	PSI Current score: 18

AGILITY
Current score: 18
	ITEMS
	  sword
	  tinderbox
	  dagger
	  lantern
	  bow and seven arrows

TREASURE *30 Gold pieces* *17* *47 Gold pieces*	*a tear in a bottle* *a four leaf clover* *cornilion ring* *Shaggy skull* *Crystal ball* *fragment of armor* *healing salves (4 times)* *salt ng tubes* *fur of a man* *Ring of Light*

ENCOUNTER BOXES

OPPONENT VIGOUR	OPPONENT VIGOUR
OPPONENT VIGOUR	OPPONENT VIGOUR
OPPONENT VIGOUR	OPPONENT VIGOUR

COMBAT

During the course of your adventure, you will often come across a monster or human enemy whom you must fight. When this happens, you will be presented with an entry something like this:

107

The Giant tears a branch from a nearby tree and lumbers towards you. There is nowhere to run – you must fight.

GIANT   VIGOUR 15

Roll two dice:

score 2 to 6   You are hit; lose 3 VIGOUR points

score 7 to 12   The Giant loses 3 VIGOUR points

If you win, turn to **273**.

At the start of every combat, you should record your opponent's VIGOUR score in an empty Encounter Box. You then begin the combat by rolling two dice, and, as indicated in the entry, deducting a number of points from either your own VIGOUR score or that of your opponent. If you and your opponent still have VIGOUR scores of more than 0, you repeat this procedure for successive *Combat Rounds*, deducting the appropriate VIGOUR points each time, until the VIGOUR

score of either you or your enemy is reduced to 0
– indicating death. Keep note of the VIGOUR
scores on your Character Sheet and in the Encounter Box.

ESCAPING FROM COMBAT

In some cases you may be engaged in combat and
find yourself losing. If given the option, you may
FLEE from the combat. Your enemy will, however,
attempt to strike a blow at your unguarded back
as you turn to run. To represent this, whenever
you choose to FLEE you should roll two dice and
compare the total to your AGILITY score. If the
dice roll *exceeds* your AGILITY then you have been
hit (losing 3 VIGOUR points) as you FLEE. If the
dice roll is *less than or equal to* your AGILITY score,
however, you dodge your opponent's parting
blow and escape without further injury.

ITEMS

You are certain to come across a number of ITEMS.
Some of these may turn out to be useless – or
even harmful – but sometimes even the most
insignificant-looking acquisition can prove vital to
your quest. You should fill in items on your
Character Sheet as you acquire them and cross
them off as they are discarded or used up.

Leaving aside such obvious possessions as your
clothing, backpack, etc, which need not be listed,
you begin with several important items. These

have already been filled in on your Character
Sheet:

your sword
a lantern
a tinder-box
30 Gold Pieces
a dagger
bow and seven arrows

THE ADVENTURE

You are now almost ready to begin. You will start
by reading the BACKGROUND, and then proceed
to 1 and thence to further entries according to the
decisions you make.

You may find it useful to take notes as you
progress through the adventure. When you enter
the Castle of Lost Souls, make a map of its rooms
and passageways. If you get killed, fill in a new
Character Sheet and start again – using your earlier
maps and notes to guide you. It may take more
than one attempt, but if you persevere you will
eventually win through to face the demon in his
fortress lair!

And now – your adventure begins . . .

BACKGROUND

Lynton is a prosperous market town that has grown rich and fat on its bustling trade. The jewellers and craftsmen of the town are without peer; its cuisine is unsurpassed for many leagues; wealthy patrons ensure a flourishing of the arts. An excellent place to visit, for someone with gold to spend . . .

You push away your breakfast platter of gruel and glower at your sagging money-pouch. Soon it will be time to move on. Lynton is, you decide, altogether *too* peaceful – no one has need of services such as yours.

There is a tall young man crossing the dew-soaked green who shares your despondent mood. 'By all the Fates!' he mutters to himself as he passes. 'Is there no adventurer of true mettle in this wretched town?' Noting the young man's fine clothes and rings, you leap up and fall into stride beside him, quickly making an introduction.

He turns and says keenly, 'I am Jasper, head of the wealthy Faze family since my father's untimely death some months ago. My brothers and I require a warrior to undertake an extremely dangerous quest. We have sent word far and wide, and many freebooters have applied for the position. In every case, their boastfulness has exceeded their courage and skill. We are on the point of despair, but i you can prove yourself worthy then you stand to profit richly.'

You accompany Jasper to the Faze mansion, an imposing edifice that stands proudly in some thirty acres of grounds. He takes you to meet his four brothers and they waste no time in beginning their stringent tests. You demonstrate your fighting skill using a wooden practice sword, effortlessly flooring Jasper's ox-like bodyguard. An archery butt is reduced to splintered wood as you send one arrow after another unerringly along the target range. When, blindfolded, you are required to dodge skittles tossed by Jasper and his brothers, your sixth sense and your co-ordination are shown to be almost superhuman. You are questioned closely on your past adventures and have no trouble listing the proper way of dealing with any monster from a basilisk to a vampire. With each test, Jasper's smile broadens. Eventually he throws down the book in which he has been keeping notes. 'Enough!' he cries. 'There can be no doubt – you are the champion we seek.'

You accompany Jasper to his study, where he explains the quest to you. 'The Castle of Lost Souls,' he begins abruptly, 'is where the demon Slank imprisons the spirits of those who pledge themselves to him.' He puts a glass of brandy into your hand; you drain it without thinking. 'My father, Luther Faze, died a wealthy man, but in his younger days he was but a struggling merchant. One day he came across an ornate bronze jar among his trinkets and wares. Unable to remember where he had got it, he read the inscription on the bottom. Immediately the arch-demon Slank stepped from out of nowhere!

'After some haggling, my father concluded a deal with Slank – to wit, that he should prosper and grow rich in order to leave wealth for his sons and a dowry for his lovely daughter. For this price the demon would have his soul.

'Father died six months ago. As you can see from this mansion and the estates, the demon kept his side of the bargain. While Father lay on his deathbed, then, Slank waited to take his soul to the Castle. None of us could see Slank, of course, but we caught the odour of damnation in the room – and Father had already told me, his eldest son, about the deal. Just as father breathed his last, a single tear fell from our sister Elvira's eyes on to his face . . .

'We learned the rest later, and I'll explain how in a moment. The demon took father's soul through low hills and swamps to where the Castle lurks enshrouded by mist. Father heard the demon chuckle as he closed the doors behind them. Gathering his courage, he turned round and cast the teardrop into Slank's face. The demon howled in pain and ran off through the Castle, clutching his eye which now sizzled and smoked where the tear struck it.

'Father was – is – no fool. Seeing that in goodness lay the means to destroy the evil demon, he barricaded himself in the Castle library and sat down to work out the necessary weapons. The action of killing Slank can be thought of as a spell which requires six components: a crystal ball, a four leaf clover, the ashes of a saint, the hair of a nun, a metal fragment from the armour of a chivalrous knight, and a tear from my sister's eyes. Luckily Father also found a book of necromancy and used its spells to appear to us in a dream. He told us what to do, and that we should seek out a bold adventurer to be the family's champion. I hardly need to say that if you can rescue our father's soul from Slank's castle, we will pay you a sizable fortune in gold and gems.'

You smile and accept. Jasper reaches into his pocket and takes out a glass phial containing a single glistening teardrop. 'Here is one of the items you will need. I wish you all speed in finding the other five.'

You take the tear (record it on your Character Sheet) and set out at once. You have an uncanny feeling that you are about to become embroiled in the strangest adventure of your life!

NOW TURN TO 1.

1

Resolving to be systematic in your quest, you decide to begin by finding the crystal ball and the four leaf clover. You remember passing an inn called The Four Leaf Clover just off the market square, and this seems as good a place as any to commence the search.

A short walk across town brings you to the inn. As you enter the tap-room, the first thing you notice is a horse brass in the shape of a four leaf clover which hangs above the bar. You may try stealing this (turn to **190**) if you think it will serve your purposes – or you could ask the innkeeper if he knows where there is some clover to be found (turn to **227**). If you prefer, you could strike up a conversation with some of the customers in the bar. Will you join a group of gypsies (turn to **56**), several farm workers having lunch (turn to **246**) or a trio of adventurers, presumably would-be champions who failed Jasper's tests (turn to **176**)?

2

At the start of the corridor you discover a naked sword hanging on a slender gold thread from the ceiling. Your lantern-light seems to dance along its razor sharp blade. You may take the sword (turn to **254**) or step under it and continue along the corridor (turn to **207**).

3

You resist the spell's effect. Seeing this, the Chonchon snarls and starts to fly away. Enraged by its noxious evil, you will not permit it to escape so easily. You unlimber your bow. Turn to **274**.

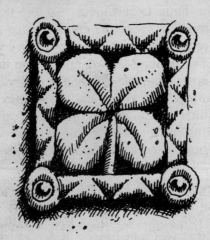

4

You are in a bewildering maze of mirror-walled passages.

To go north	Turn to **51**
To go south	Turn to **64**
To go east	Turn to **17**
To go west	Turn to **12**

5

You toss the three coins down on the floor in front of you. One lands with the unicorn's head uppermost, the other two with the serpent's head. Does that give you any ideas? You can retrieve the coins if you wish, then turn back to **147** and choose which door to open.

6

The path up into the Mungo Hills takes you along a ridge overlooking a valley. As you walk, you notice a stone idol down in the valley. Will you detour to inspect it (turn to **191**) or carry on along the path (turn to **301**)?

7

You open the phial and allow the tear to fall into your own eye, thinking perhaps that it will show you the true route to the castle. Unfortunately, this does not work – and you have now used the teardrop (remove it from your Character Sheet). You grit your teeth and trudge on towards where the castle seems to be. Turn to **84**.

8

You dip your hand into the pool and take the bottle. Will you remove the stopper from it now?

If so, turn to **216**. If not, note it down on your Character Sheet and turn to **126**.

9

You stumble on, only to trip over a clump of turf and fall flat on your face in the mud. Picking yourself up, you scowl, set your jaw and start trudging doggedly towards the distant castle. As fast as you walk, it seems to recede from you. As last you decide to look for inspiration in your backpack. Turn to **62**.

10

'Oh. Well, at least you must have the ashes of a saint?' If you do, turn to **275**. If not, turn to **88**.

11

You throw the four coins down to him. He snatches them from the air and pockets them with one fluid sweep of his arm. You may now continue on your way (turn to **6**) or ask him if he knows where you can get the last two items you need (turn to **236**).

12

You climb the steps of the brightly painted cara-van, push aside the silk curtain across the door-way, and cautiously enter. It is dimly lit. There is

a strange herbal smell – incense, perhaps? Exotic and colourful fabrics hang down in drapes, disguising the size of the caravan's interior. You feel heady and disorientated, as though you have stepped from the noise and bustle outside into another world.

As your eyes adjust to the gloom, you notice with a start a figure who sits at a velvet covered table. She is clad in the same brilliant colours that adorn the caravan. You are pleasantly surprised to discover that Gypsy Gayl is no wizened crone, but a ravishing sultry beauty with red-gold hair and long-lashed eyes of sea green. She beckons you forward. Finally you notice her crystal ball on the table. It shimmers and reflects all the myriad colours in the room.

You have fleetingly considered several plans, and now must decide which to use. Will you:

Ask her to tell your fortune?	Turn to 52
Suggest she reads her own fortune?	Turn to 162
Try to steal her crystal ball?	Turn to 263
Invite her to join you in a drink and spend some time looking around the fete?	Turn to 58

13

You grudgingly hand him seven Gold Pieces. Remember to deduct them from the total cash on your Character Sheet. You may now pass by and continue on your way (turn to **6**) or ask him where you could find the two items you still need (turn to **236**).

14

Gayl has retreated to the shadows at the rear of the caravan. Her eyes glint at you from the near-darkness. You wipe the gore from your sword on the velvet tablecloth and lift the crystal ball from its stand. When you bid her farewell, she spits on the floor and rasps something unpleasant in her own language. You leave quickly before she can work her witchcraft upon you. Turn to **208**.

15

He lies slain at your feet. You snatch up the helmet and shoulder your way through the ring of astonished onlookers. No one tries to stop you, as you have bested this perfect if not exactly gentle knight. You chip off the fragment you require and then throw the helmet into a ditch. Turn to **269**.

16

Do you have the Wristband of Lightning? If so, turn to **112**. If not, an electrical discharge as you try to step into the alcove hurls you back across the room. Deduct 4 points from your VIGOUR score. If you are still alive you decide to leave and continue along the corridor – turn to **192**.

The door seems to be barred or barricaded shut. If you wish to knock, turn to **180**. Otherwise, you may try the door in the other wall (turn to **264**) or carry on to the end of the corridor (turn to **135**).

18

You pull the folds of the rug around you. It is comfortably warm and you are glad you had the foresight to bring it with you. Will you now try to get at the mask (turn to **41**), or leave through the archway (turn to **288**)?

19

A musty odour of mouldered bones and cerements rises from the sarcophagus as you push the heavy lid to the floor. You lift your lantern and peer within. Amid the layers of dust, the only item that has survived the ravages of time is a tarnished crown. Rubies sparkle around its rim. You may take the crown and place it on your head (turn to **289**), or leave it and carry on – either through the archway (turn to **234**) or along the passage you were in before (turn to **44**).

20

Roll one die. If you score 4 or less, turn to **265**. If you score 5 or 6, turn to **89**.

21

She has powerful sorcery at her beck and call, but you resist its effects and hurry away before she is able to prepare another spell. Turn to **208**.

22

It takes real courage to attack a Mountain Lion. No brains, just courage . . .

LION   VIGOUR 15

Roll two dice:
score 2 to 7   You are wounded; lose 3 VIGOUR
score 8 to 12   The Lion loses 3 VIGOUR

After three Combat Rounds you have a chance to FLEE past it; turn to **24** if you do. If you kill it, turn to **255**.

23

You step into a shadowy, cloistered hallway that reeks of funeral incense. All is bathed in the guttering, smoky light of myriad black candles. A wide staircase leads up to the first floor. Over to one side of the hallway you see double doors carved with arabesque designs. Will you open the doors (turn to **73**), or proceed up the stairs (turn to **103**)?

24

You walk on, maintaining a good pace. Pausing only briefly for lunch, you are on your way down out of the hills by mid-afternoon. Ahead of you, the trail forks in two. One way will take you into the Swamps of Bosh (where you are headed), but the other presumably leads to the notorious Dragonbreath Canyon (where you definitely do not want to go). Beside the fork there is a large flat rock on which squat two tiny shrivelled goblins with large heads and a shock of white hair over their sharp, wily faces.

'Are you a Dran or a Kabbagoo?' you ask the first goblin as you stride up to them. He answers so indistinctly that you cannot hear him, but then the second goblin pipes up: 'He said he's a Kabbagoo. Are you deaf or something?' Ignoring his disrespectful attitude, you demand of the second goblin which route you should take to reach the Swamps of Bosh. 'Swamps of Bosh?' he

replies. 'You want to go left.' As you set off, he calls after you: 'Go on, push off to Bosh!' Both goblins start giggling, but you cannot be bothered to go back and teach them a lesson. Which path will you take now – the left-hand one as suggested (turn to **202**), or the right-hand one (turn to **217**)?

25

There is no way to tell for certain, but somehow you feel you must be making some progress. As you arrive at the next junction, your choice of path is more confident.

To go north	Turn to **51**
To go south	Turn to **197**
To go east	Turn to **43**
To go west	Turn to **4**

26

You dive forward, but your blow encounters no resistance. You plunge through the curtain into an empty alcove, and as you are struggling to disentangle yourself from the thick folds of velvet you feel a keen blade bite into your shoulder. Lose 3 VIGOUR points. If you are still alive, you stagger around to confront the evil little Dwarf who has just attacked you. He dances from one stockinged foot to the other, cackling gleefully, as you advance towards him. Turn to **81**.

You advance along a narrow corridor illuminated by the amber glow of oil lamps. Shortly you come to a door in the left-hand wall. A few metres further, on the other side of the corridor, you see another door. Will you:

Try the door to your left?	Turn to **17**
Try the door to your right?	Turn to **264**
Continue along the corridor	Turn to **135**

28

One falls, but the others fight on. They circle so quickly, occasionally lunging towards you with a taunting feint, that you cannot keep your eyes on all of them at once.

Roll two dice:

score 2 to 3	You are hit three times; lose 9 VIGOUR
score 4 to 5	You are hit twice; lose 6 VIGOUR
score 6 to 7	You are hit once; lose 3 VIGOUR
score 8 to 12	One of them (you decide whom) loses 3 VIGOUR

If you FLEE now, lose 9 VIGOUR points if you fail the AGILITY roll – turn to **219**. If you fight on and kill another robber, turn to **128**.

29

Somehow you manage to drag yourself the last few yards and slump through the archway. The coldness is presumably a magical effect restricted to the last room, for after a few minutes you stop shivering and manage to get to your feet. Rubbing the circulation back into your sword-hand, you look around you. Turn to **288**.

30

You have gone on only about a hundred metres when you suddenly come upon all your missing equipment. It is lying in a neat pile directly in front of you. Delighted at this happy change in your fortunes, you gather up the items and replace them in your backpack before continuing on your way with a spring in your step and a merry tune on your lips. Turn to **221**.

31

The Cobra draws back from your flashing blade, hissing angrily. You watch as its head begins to sway to and fro. The darkness begins to cloud around you, a stygian blackness through which the serpent's golden eyes burn like molten gems. Attempt to roll equal to or less than your *current* PSI score on two dice. If you succeed, turn to **248**. If you fail, turn to **165**.

The mask is so cold that it burns your fingers. You try to wrap it in your cloak, but you can still feel the unnatural chill of it sapping your body heat. You cannot take it with you then. Will you take an item from your backpack (turn to **181**), or leave the room (turn to **288**)?

You are fighting an Undine – a water elemental. Every time it strikes you, you must roll equal to or less than your *current* PSI score on two dice. If you fail this roll, the Undine saps some of your resistance to magic and you must reduce your *current* PSI score by 1.

UNDINE   VIGOUR **9**

Roll two dice:
score 2 to 7   You are struck; lose 3 VIGOUR and roll as explained above
score 8 to 12   The Undine loses 3 VIGOUR

If your PSI score is reduced to 0, turn to **116**. If you win, turn to **8**.

By the time you reach the tree, the strands of hair are no longer there. Or perhaps they were never

there in the first place . . . You continue on your way. Turn to **221**.

35

You awaken with a start, instantly aware of danger. You hurl yourself to one side just as an axe crashes down. A fraction slower and your skull would have been split like firewood! You find your sword. Facing you in the half-light is Garl, wielding the massive axe as though it were barely more than a toothpick. Turn to **295**.

36

You walk around the field where the joust is taking place. Amongst the various knights parading back and forth on horseback or cuffing their indolent squires you see a very gallant looking knight with a noble lady. Using the most courtly and chivalrous phrases, he is declaring his boundless love for her. She offers him a band of green silk finished with gold – the symbol of her favour – and he accepts with a self-effacing smile. You have found your man. You approach him. Will you:

Explain your quest and ask for his help?	Turn to **185**
Steal his helmet when he isn't looking?	Turn to **50**
Resort to low cunning?	Turn to **261**

37

You dash out of the inn and down a side alley.
You still have the horse brass in your pocket, and
you are also fairly sure that none of the people got
a good look at you in the gloom of the tap-room.
You regret having been forced to kill one of them,
but you were after all acting in self-defence. Turn
to **124**.

38

One of the curtains is thrown back as you pass,
and a crazed Dwarf emerges from the alcove in
which he was waiting to ambush you. You observe
that he has no boots on his feet; clearly he lef
them under the curtains opposite as a wily ruse
Fortunately you were not taken in. Turn to **81**.

39

You slip the brass into your pocket a fraction of
second before the innkeeper turns to take you
order. You smile absent-mindedly and tell hin
you have forgotten your money-pouch. While h
fingers his jaw suspiciously you saunter out int
the street. Turn to **273**.

40

'Churls with no lawfulness or honour roam o
highways,' the captain continues. 'The time h

come to deal harshly with all who would defy the rule of law. My own orders are to administer immediate punishment to any lawbreakers I encounter.' There is a fanatical gleam in his eyes as he rants on, and he ignores your attempts to change the topic of conversation. You begin to squirm uncomfortably in your chair. Suddenly you realize that he is talking about the recent murder of one of the king's toll-collectors. You reach back slowly for the sword behind you, but your arm is seized and twisted roughly. The soldiers pin you down as their captain approaches, dagger in hand.

He acts in the name of justice but, in truth, his imagination proves much more evil than yours. Your end is not a pleasant one . . .

41

You attack the ice with your knifeblade, but it is refreezing as fast as you can chip it away. If you are determined to reach the mask you will have to think of something else to try – turn to **125**. If you are ready to give up and go through the archway, turn to **288**.

42

They look at one another. 'Maybe the hermit will have some,' suggests one of them. 'Can't say for sure,' another tells you – 'but he collects just about anything.' They stand up and take you off to meet him. Turn to **286**.

43

You stand at a crossroads. Identical mirrored passages lead off in the cardinal directions.

To go north	Turn to **51**
To go south	Turn to **64**
To go east	Turn to **179**
To go west	Turn to **121**

44

Before long you emerge into a curtained gallery with a single door at the far end. A trapdoor is set into the middle of the floor. If you wish to open the trapdoor, turn to **96**. If you wish to walk along the gallery and go through the door at the end, turn to **308**.

45

Slank is using his foul magic to try and persuade you to serve him, but no demon will ever corrupt an honourable and undaunting spirit like yours. Grimly, you push the curtain aside. Turn to **46**.

46

Did you leave either the clover or the teardrop on Slank's mask? If so, turn to **204**. If not, turn to **282**.

47

You rise early and take breakfast with Jasper. His brothers are still in bed, and the mansion seems eerily quiet. Hardly a word passes between the two of you; Jasper knows he may be sending you to your death, and the coffers of gold he has promised appear a paltry reward now. The door creaks behind you and the butler enters with your weapons and backpack. 'I have had Mortlake pack some provisions for your journey,' says Jasper. 'And you will also find in your rucksack a small pot containing four applications of a magical Salve of Healing.'

The Salve of Healing is a rather foul-smelling preparation made from rancid milk, troll fat and rotting vegetables which actually has miraculous healing properties. Spreading it on your wounds after a fight will restore 4 VIGOUR points; the

Salve will not increase your VIGOUR above its *normal* score, of course. Record the Salve of Healing on your Character Sheet – and remember you have only enough for four applications.

You take up your belongings and Jasper accompanies you to the mansion gates. 'I wish you good luck in your venture,' he tells you as you walk. 'I can offer you no help or advice save these two snippets of information. First, I have heard that the two principal goblin tribes of the Mungo Hills, through which you must pass, are the Drans and the Kabbagoos and that one or the other tribe are inveterate liars. Secondly, it is said that strange phantasms can appear in the mists enveloping the Swamps of Bosh which surround Slank's castle. These phantasms can cause a traveller no hardship so long as one disregards them.' He reaches up and removes a talisman from around his neck which he hands to you. 'Wear this, for if you find my father he will recognize it and know that you come to help him.' He swings the gate open and offers you his hand. 'Now, farewell!'

You make your way through the town towards the west gate. The streets are beginning to come alive with traders laying out their wares. Sunlight slants across the rooftops and there is a cool refreshing breeze. Somewhere on your journey you must find a saint's ashes and the hair of a nun – but for now all that occupies your thoughts is that it is a glorious morning and you are about to embark on another challenging adventure. Turn to **205**.

The room consists of a hexagonal main chamber with a large alcove off the far end. Hanging on the wall in the alcove you can see a gilded longsword decorated with rubies. As you step closer, you notice an acrid smell in the room and a blue-white flickering across the alcove entrance. Will you step into the alcove (turn to **16**), or leave and continue along the corridor (turn to **192**)?

49

If you have offered at least three Gold Pieces, the armourer dourly pockets the bribe and shaves off a sliver of armour for you. You hide the fragment under your tunic and return the breastplate to the knight. Turn to **269**.

If you offered the armourer two Gold Pieces or less, turn to **74**.

50

You creep up to where his saddle, lance and helmet lie unattended on the grass. While his squire snores happily, you gently lift the helmet and start to skulk off with it under your arm. But luck is not with you – you trip over the guy-rope of a tent and fall heavily. The knight turns and sees you. With a single bound he is upon you, sword glinting in the morning sunlight. You have no choice but to fight.

Roll two dice:

score 2 to 6   You are wounded; lose 3
                 VIGOUR
score 7 to 12   The Knight loses 3 VIGOUR

If you win, turn to **15**. If you decide to submit, turn to **174**.

51

The passage stretches on and finally brings you to a crossroads. Which way will you go from here:

North?	Turn to **170**
South?	Turn to **107**
East?	Turn to **43**
West?	Turn to **249**

52

If you have any money left, you must cross her palm with a Gold Piece. She gazes into her crystal ball. There she sees much of your past and a little of your future. A soft smile plays on her lips. 'Your intentions are clear to me,' she says. 'If you desire my crystal ball you must pay more than gold for it . . .'

Suddenly she draws a slender dagger and pricks your finger with the point of it. A single droplet of dark blood falls on to the ball and seems to be absorbed into its glistening surface. You reel with momentary weakness; you have permanently lost point from your *normal* VIGOUR score. A Salve of Healing will not restore this, and nor will anything else. In exchange for the drop of life-blood, Gayl gives you a second crystal ball which he takes from a casket behind her. You accept it and leave, feeling you have indeed paid dearly for his item. Turn to **208**.

53

ou lift the ladle and sip a little of the mixture. oll five dice – if you score equal to or less than our *current* VIGOUR score turn to **163**. If you core greater than your VIGOUR, turn to **71**.

54

ne of your opponents falls, and you now have e chance to FLEE from the inn if you wish. Turn 273 if you do. If you prefer to continue the ght:

Roll two dice:
score 2 to 4   You are hit; lose 3 VIGOUR
score 5 to 12   Your opponent loses 3 VIGOUR

If you win, turn to **145**.

55

fter almost an hour you have still not got any oser to your destination. It is obviously time to try something else, and you search in your back-pack for inspiration. Turn to **62**.

56

You pay two Gold Pieces for a bottle of wine and take it over to where they are sitting. As you fill their goblets, you introduce yourself. They smile and nod, but say nothing. What will you ask them first – if they know where you can find a crystal ball (turn to **97**) or a four leaf clover (turn to **209**)? If you chose to be circumspect, you might ask if they could introduce you to a fortune teller (turn to **154**).

57

The others stare aghast as a second man falls victim to a powerful thrust of your sword. Their faces are pale, and as you step forward they throw down their makeshift weapons and run in terror. None of the other patrons of the inn seems inclined to challenge you. You go back to the bar, quickly finish your drink and hurry from the inn. Turn to **124**.

58

She is flattered and accepts with a gay smile. You leave the caravan together and make your way to a large tent nearby. A few drunken figures – townsfolk and gypsies alike – stand, sit and lie around it. The wine and ale flow freely here. You push your way through the crowds of merry-makers and find a small table, where you begin to ply Gayl with drinks. Soon she relaxes and starts to laugh and joke. A few of the more rowdy revellers egg her on to dance for them. Someone pushes a tamborine into her hand. She leaps up and slaps it against her thigh as she whirls in a sensual dance. The men all cheer, crowding in a circle around her and clapping their hands. You enjoy a last sip of wine, then make a discreet exit. Returning to her caravan, you take the crystal ball and slip away from the fete. Turn to **208**.

59

Your opponent is panting for breath now, but you are getting your second wind. You move forward, hoping to finish him quickly.

Roll two dice:

score 2 to 4   You are wounded; lose 3 VIGOUR

score 5 to 12   The robber loses 3 VIGOUR

If you win, turn to **223**. If you FLEE even now, turn to **219**.

60

Since it is now getting late you start to look around for somewhere to make camp. You soon find a patch of high ground that is fairly dry. Using the

wood you collected earlier, you soon have a good fire going. After a light supper you settle down and go to sleep.

You come awake suddenly. Hours have passed – the fire is just glowing embers now. Creatures are stirring in the darkness all around you. Slowly you sit up, Your camp is surrounded by hordes of Marshons – small, hairless leathery creatures with webbed hands and large, lidless eyes. They have been attracted by your fire and the starlight glimmering off your sword, which is skewered in the ground beside you. Marshons usually see only the dull sludge greens and greys of the swamp, so they are instantly drawn by light and colour. They move around you like moths around a candle. From what you have heard they eat only fungus and swampweed – but nonetheless you are in the most deadly peril for, if they press forward towards the light, you will be smothered and crushed by the countless hundreds of them. What will you do? You may toss your sword away in the hope that they will scurry after it (turn to 280), or light your lantern (turn to 210), or – if you have one – you could use a Ring of Light (turn to 178).

61

Though you believe your actions were justified, the gods rank you as a murderer. They do not want their shrine sullied by your presence. They despatch one of their servants to deal with you – a giant, halberd-wielding warrior clad in white armour who steps from a shining rent in the air in front of you. You are so taken aback by his sudden and miraculous appearance that you get no chance to drink a potion (if you have any).

ANGELIC EXECUTIONER   VIGOUR 15

Roll two dice:

score 2 to 6   You are wounded and lose 3
                  VIGOUR
score 7 to 12   The Executioner loses 3
                  VIGOUR

If you FLEE back to the path and head west, turn to **301**. If you beat the Executioner, he turns into a stream of clear water and flows away – turn to **243**.

62

Which of your items will you use? Perhaps the four leaf clover (turn to **65**), the little girl's teardrop (turn to **7**) or the gypsy's crystal ball (turn to **242**).

63

Human torsos dripping with gore hang on rusted meathooks along the larder walls. You can see maggots crawling on some of them. Slank obviously likes game adventurers. Ranged on wooden shelves you see a number of jars and bottles. You lean closer to read the faded labels; they contain all manner of ingredients. There is a jar of newts' eyes, another of frogs' toes, one contains a pickled dog's tongue and the next holds fillet of fen snake. One bottle has no label, but its contents are unmistakably lizard legs. Among the more normal ingredients, you notice red pepper, parsley and salt. You can take up to three jars if you wish – note them down on your Character Sheet. Feeling your gorge rise at the sight and stench of the demon's awful larder, you continue on your way (turn to **240**).

64

The mirrored passages sprawl in a seemingly endless array all around you. You find yourself at a four-way intersection, from which you may go:

North	Turn to **170**
South	Turn to **107**
East	Turn to **43**
West	Turn to **179**

65

Some people claim that a four leaf clover placed under the tongue prevents one from speaking anything but the truth. This old wives' tale can be of no use to you here. You replace the clover in your backpack and trudge on in the direction you imagine the castle to lie. Turn to **84**.

66

You drift back off to sleep and pass the rest of the night in comfort – except for the clouds of gnats and the occasional far-off howl of a moorland monster. You wake at dawn. If you are wounded, add 1 point to your *current* VIGOUR score for the rest. You eat a hearty breakfast and then press on deeper into Bosh. Turn to **79**.

67

You scramble frantically up the cliff. A deep voice calls up from below; to your astonishment, the lion can talk! 'Now look here,' it says, 'for one thing I can jump that high anyway, so you might as well come down. More importantly, I seem to have this bloody great thorn thing stuck right through my paw.' You see that this is indeed true. If you wish to climb down to help the beast, turn to **173**. If you decide to stay where you are, turn to **167**.

68

He offers you a Luck Charm for 20 Gold Pieces. If you decline this and continue to wander around the fete, turn to **140**. If you buy the Charm, pay him the 20 Gold Pieces and turn to **225**.

69

You trek on towards the castle, but every time you glance away from it you look up to find it has shifted to a different location. Nor do you seem to be getting any closer. You decide it is time to try using one of your items, and open your backpack. Turn to **62**.

70

A line of images stretches in infinite reflection to either side of you. Eventually you reach another four-way intersection. Will you go:

North?	Turn to **51**
South?	Turn to **64**
East?	Turn to **25**
West?	Turn to **4**

The effect of the brew hits you like a poleaxe and you fall to the floor. This is the favourite soup of the demon, but to any mortal it is a virulent poison. The life ebbs from your pain-wracked body. Your quest has ended in failure.

You set out at a brisk pace and soon leave the fields and meadows around the town far behind you. After some time you come to a river and, seeing a bridge only a few hundred metres away, you stroll along the bank to it. As you are about to cross, however, a tall slim man in silver-grey robes appears from under the arch of the bridge and calls up to you that you must pay a toll of four Gold Pieces to cross here. Will you pay him the money (turn to 11), or will you ignore him and cross anyway (turn to 230)?

Beyond the double doors you see a dimly lit room. A pine torch burns in a bracket on the wall. The same heavy incense you noticed before lingers here. At the far end of the room you can just make out a darkened archway. There is blackness beyond. Will you return to the hallway and go upstairs (turn to 103), or cross the room to the archway (turn to 111)?

74

He sneers, finishes his work on the breastplate, and carries it back to the knight himself. Furious, you storm from the tournament field and resolve to obtain the fragment you need from the armour collection of Hrothgar the scholar. Turn to **152**.

75

The other Gypsy lunges at you over the fallen body of his brother. Hatred fills his eyes, and Gayl screams at him to slay you.

Second GYPSY   VIGOUR 12

Roll two dice:
score 2 to 5   You are hit; lose 3 VIGOUR
score 6 to 12   The Gypsy loses 3 VIGOUR

If you win, turn to **14**.

76

You climb through the bedroom window and escape into the night. You trek for several miles with only the wan moonlight to guide you. When you stop to check your belongings, you are distressed to find that you left behind one of the items you collected in the hurry to get away. Cross one of the following from your Character Sheet: a nun's hair, a teardrop in a vial, a saint's ashes in an urn, a four leaf clover or a fragment of armour.

You have also lost your money pouch. Cold, tired and impoverished, then, you drift into a restless slumber and awake early the next morning, anxious to be on your way. Turn to **132**.

77

You can wager up to three Gold Pieces (decide how much now) on either a proudly strutting bantam or his opponent, who is larger but has a tattered comb. If you choose the former, turn to **99**. If the latter, turn to **247**.

78

Your arrow wings the Chonchon's ear and it plummets from the sky. You walk leisurely over to where it has fallen. The arrow has torn through its ear but it is still alive and thrashing. You grind it into the mud with the heel of your boot. Noticing a gold ring through its left ear, you take out your dagger and cut this free. The ring is large enough to fit around your wrist and is in fact a Wristband of Lightning. Note this down on your Character Sheet before turning to **222**.

79

As you walk on, a few tendrils of mist return to swirl about you. You do not mind now; the mist is almost like an old travelling companion. Certainly, it uses no more illusions . . .

Then, in the distance, you see the Castle of Lost Souls. Unless it is another of the mist's apparitions, it cannot be more than a few miles away! You head towards it. However, when you look up again after going only a few hundred yards, you find that the castle is no longer straight ahead of you. You walk towards it for almost an hour, keeping your eyes on it the whole time, but you do not seem to be getting any closer. Presumably the demon Slank has set enchantments around his castle to keep unwelcome visitors away, so what will you do now? If you wish to just continue marching towards the castle, keeping your eyes fixed on it continually so it does not change location again, turn to **91**. If you wish to use an item from your backpack, turn to **62**. If you would like to try something else, turn to **138**.

80

You stand over the fallen body for several minutes, half expecting Slank to rise a second time, and ready to renew the battle at once if he does. But he used the last of his sorcerous power against you; this time he stays dead. Turn to **309**.

81

Snarling monstrous oaths, the horrible Dwarf swings his axe and rushes forward to strike at you.

DWARF

Roll two dice:

score 2 to 5   You are hit; lose 3 VIGOUR
score 6 to 12   The Dwarf loses 3 VIGOUR

If you FLEE through the door at the end of the gallery, turn to **220**. If you kill the Dwarf, turn to **238**.

82

You stand in a sacred place. The gods themselves look into your heart and see your past deeds. If you have slain anyone at all in your quest so far (except for a fat cutpurse at the fête), turn to **61**. If you have got this far without killing a soul – apart from the fat cutpurse, if you encountered him – turn to **243**.

83

By pouring salt over the ice you lower its freezing point; it starts to melt, and you now have little difficulty in digging down to the mask with your knife. Turn to **100**.

84

As you go on, a soft low beating drifts across the barren moors. You listen to the sound and it seems to form words – *slay, slay slay* . . .

You look up to see four dark shapes swooping

down through the mist towards you. The creatures attacking you are Chonchons. These disembodied heads fly using their large veined ears as wings and attack by biting with their chisel-like teeth. Three of them fly in to engage you: *fight them one at a time*.

First CHONCHON   VIGOUR 6
Second CHONCHON   VIGOUR 6
Third CHONCHON   VIGOUR 6

Roll two dice:
score 2 to 5   You are bitten; lose 2 VIGOUR
score 6 to 12   The Chonchon you are fighting
                loses 3 VIGOUR

If you are still fighting at least one of the Chonchons after seven Combat Rounds, turn to **283**. If you kill all three before this, turn to **253**.

85

You pour a little of the oil from your lantern on to the surface of the pool, thereby calming the troubled waters. The Undine immediately becomes quiescent and sinks back into the pool. You cautiously dip your hand into the still water to take the bottle. If you wish to unstopper this now, turn to **216**. If not, note it down on your Character Sheet and turn to **126**.

86

One of your assailants stumbles a few paces and

then falls dead. The others are too enraged now to break off the fight.

Roll two dice:

score 2 to 4	You are hit twice – lose 6 VIGOUR
score 5 to 6	You are hit once and lose 3 VIGOUR
score 7 to 12	You inflict a 3 VIGOUR wound on one of them (you decide which)

If you defeat another, turn to **175**.

87

'Can't say for a fact,' says one, 'but another drink might jog our memories.' They all chortle and finger their stubbly beards expectantly. If you wish to buy them another round of drinks, cross off another three Gold Pieces and turn to **213**. If you prefer to try your luck with one of the other groups in the tap-room, turn to **117**.

88

Luther shrugs. 'Too bad. Still, maybe you can finish Slank off anyway – you'll just need to be that much more careful. Now, I wish you good luck.' He shows you to the library door and the two of you shake hands. As you continue along the corridor you can hear him replacing the barricade on the other side of the door. Turn to **134**.

89

It is exhausting work, but you eventually manage to dig the mask out of the ice. Turn to **100**.

90

You make your way back up into the Mungo Hills. The two goblins are very amused to see you returning – so much so that one of them declares between giggles that he is a Kabbagoo. You travel on eastwards and, late in the afternoon of the second day, arrive back at the town. Jasper is furious. He berates you for your incompetence in losing all the items and finally dismisses you. Your reputation in tatters, you gather your belongings and slink from the town. You have failed.

91

As you trudge on through the dull murky greyness, you see a darkness on the horizon beyond the castle. You find yourself walking against a freezing wind. The storm is moving towards you – the whole sky blackens as the clouds billow up from the horizon and icy white stripes advance to hide the castle from view. Hailstones the size of a man's fist pound down all around you. If you cannot find refuge from the storm quickly you will be pummelled to death. Even the mist disperses, taking shelter wherever it may. One of the tendrils of mist drifts down into the ground, where you see a hole like the burrow of a large animal. If it is truly a burrow then you may have to fight its occupant – but that is certainly better than standing here, waiting to be battered to death by the hailstones. With one hand on the pommel of your blade, you descend into the hole. Turn to **232**.

92

The shadows of night are closing in as you enter the rolling, dusty landscape of the Mungo Hills. High on a ridge you see a ramshackle hut with a narrow twisting path wending up to it. If you wish to seek shelter for the night with whoever lives in the hut, turn to **146**. If you would rather make camp out here in the open, turn to **296**.

93

The passage brings you to another intersection. Again, you must choose to go one of four ways.

North	Turn to **170**
South	Turn to **107**
East	Turn to **70**
West	Turn to **121**

94

The snake's venom reaches your heart at last, and you stumble to your knees as an excruciating pain wracks you. Your chest seems as though it is about to burst open, and each breath you take is like a gulp of hot oil. You cannot prevent your muscles from stiffening into a deathly rigor. Slowly, your adventure and your life draw to a tortured close . . .

95

As you quaff the potion, a burst of energy erupts through your veins. If you are wounded, you regain 6 points of VIGOUR. Your VIGOUR is not increased above its *normal* score, of course. You discard the empty bottle. Return to the last entry you were reading.

96

You swing the trapdoor open. Immediately there is the sound of powerful springs uncoiling and a mechanical warrior jumps up into view, flailing at you with its armoured fists.

CLOCKWORK AUTOMATON   VIGOUR 12

Roll two dice:
score 2 to 6   You are struck; lose 3 VIGOUR
score 7 to 12   The Automaton loses 3
                 VIGOUR

Its mechanism is gradually running down, so after one Combat Round you may add 1 to the dice roll, after two Combat Rounds, add 2 to the dice roll, and so on. If you are still fighting after six

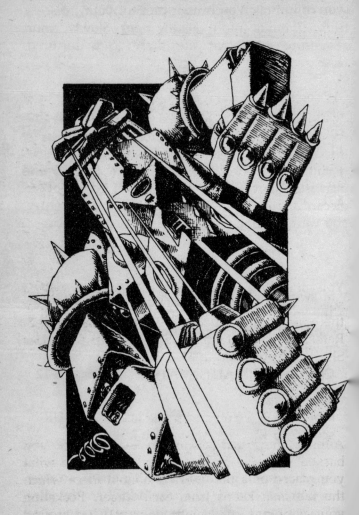

Rounds, turn to **136**. If you defeat it before then you continue on your way (turn to **308**).

97

As soon as you mention the item you seek, their expressions become guarded. One of them pushes the wine bottle across to you and invites you to drink. The others exchange sly glances as he proposes a toast. If you wish to go on drinking and chatting with them, turn to **171**. If not, turn to **131**.

98

You empty the ashes into the 'hole' and, with a sound very like a cough, it spits you out into the open. Luckily the hailstorm has now passed. Remember to cross the ashes off your Character Sheet and then turn to **69**.

99

After a short and vicious battle, the cock you backed wins the fight. You get back twice what you placed as a bet – less one Gold Piece which the tall man keeps from each wager. Pocketing your winnings, you make your way on around the fete. Turn to **129**.

100

The mask is of black-lacquered wood decorated with silver, and is a possibly fanciful represen-tation of a demon's face. You have seen its like at several masquerade parties, although never crafted with such chilling effectiveness as this. Curiously, the mask has only one eye – the left – and that has a quartz lens set into it. Will you touch the mask (turn to **32**), take out one of your items (turn to **181**), or depart through the dark archway (turn to **288**)?

101

You walk along a short tunnel and enter a circular room with a pool in the middle. There is one other exit from the room – a door to your left. You can go back and take one of the other doors – either the one with the copper plaque (turn to **279**) or the one with the bronze plaque (turn to **300**) – or you can advance across this room (turn to **114**).

102

You arise before daybreak and join the nuns in the first service of the day – as much from politeness as from piety. You also notice a group of soldiers praying in the chapel. You did not see them when you arrived yesterday, and as you file out of the chapel you strike up a conversation with their captain. He confirms that they arrived during the night. 'Patrols on the western roads have been doubled,' he tells you over breakfast. 'The countryside hereabouts is rife with brigands and murderous monsters.'

Do you have a jade horn-shaped amulet? If so, turn to **40**. If not, turn to **306**.

103

You climb up to the first floor landing. From here you can go left (turn to **27**) or right (turn to **284**).

104

You leave the clover in the mouth of the demon mask. That should prevent Slank from touching Remember to cross it off your Character Sheet. You trudge across the icy floor to the archway and step through. Turn to **288**.

105

You search their bodies and find fifteen Gold

Pieces and a Potion of Strength. You may drink the potion at the start of any combat; it will augment your strength so that each wound you inflict on an opponent will deduct 4 VIGOUR points rather than the usual 3 points. The potion's effect will last only as long as the combat for which you drink it, and there is only enough in the bottle for one use. Record these acquisitions on your Character Sheet. Whistling cheerfully, you set off back towards the town. Turn to **287**.

106

You go over to the bar and, while the innkeeper is busy polishing a glass, reach up to remove the horse brass from the wall. Roll one die. If you score a 1 or 2, turn to **270**. If you score 3 or higher turn to **39**.

107

You are standing at the junction of four seemingly indistinguishable passages, and you must decide which way to go. Will it be:

North?	Turn to **51**
South?	Turn to **64**
East?	Turn to **17**
West?	Turn to **12**

108

You stand at the very threshold of the Castle of Lost Souls. The mists of the swamp seem to shrink away from it. Its presence is awesome – you cannot grasp any sense of its size; it seems endless, eternal . . . The walls tower dizzyingly above you into the glowering, slate-grey sky. Perhaps in the castle's unreal and inhuman architecture you glean something of the twisted mind of its master, the demon Slank. The darkened slits of windows stare menacingly out across the silent marshlands. You notice a twinkling light. A solitary candle burns in one of the windows – to the left of the doorway, apparently on the first floor. All else is shrouded in darkness.

The castle is not guarded; none of the tortured souls that enter ever leaves. With weapon in hand you advance slowly across the drawbridge. You reach out – does your hand tremble just a little now? – and push open the heavy mahogany door. Turn to **23**.

(illustration on previous page)

109

You catch sight of the glint of a knife as the fat man tries to cut the strings of your money pouch. Your blood boils and you pull your sword from its scabbard with a bellow of rage. The Cutpurse attempts to escape by running between two tents, but a pile of crates blocks his way and he has to turn and face your wrath.

| CUTPURSE | VIGOUR 9 |

Roll two dice:

| score 2 to 4 | You are wounded; lose 3 VIGOUR |
| score 5 to 12 | The Cutpurse loses 3 VIGOUR |

If you win, turn to **237**.

110

You deftly slip the brass into your tunic just as the innkeeper looks up. You smile and pay him a Gold Piece, coolly finish your beer and stroll out of the inn. Turn to **124**.

111

Before you can go any further you will need a source of light. Will you take down the pine torch (turn to **120**), or would you prefer to light up your lantern (turn to **241**)?

112

An incandescent bolt arcs across the alcove entrance as you step through it, but the energy is absorbed by your Wristband and you are unharmed. The sword hangs on the wall before you. The rubies glitter and the metal gleams in the wan light of two braziers to either side of the alcove. As you reach for the sword, thick smoke billows up from these braziers and coagulates into

a dark serpentine form in the air above your head. With a shock, you realize this smoke-creature is alive and intent on fighting you!

RAUCHWURM   VIGOUR 12

Roll two dice:

score 2 to 5   You are wounded; lose 3 VIGOUR

score 6 to 12   The Rauchwurm loses 3 VIGOUR

If you FLEE back to the corridor and continue on your way, turn to **192**. If you defeat the smoke-being, turn to **231**.

113

A little further along the corridor you come to a large oak portal with an iron latch in the shape of a bat. You push it open and survey the room beyond. Directly opposite you is a high arch leading from the room. Staring down from above this arch is a rather noxious bas relief of a sneering inhuman face.

A low whimpering draws your attention to the occupant of the room – presumably one of the poor souls Slank torments for his pleasure. She is a slender woman with light brown hair, her wrists bound by leather thongs to a wooden beam above her head. Her feet rest on a red-hot metal plate. You can see the sick ingenuity of the arrangement – she is able to lift her legs clear of the plate, but eventually her arms ache so much that she has to stand on it again and get burned. She sees you and starts pleading for you to release her. If you do so, turn to **228**. If not, turn to **187**.

114

You notice a bottle of grey-green glass at the bottom of the pool. Before you can decide whether to reach in and take it or not, the surface of the pool starts rippling and heaving like a lake in a storm. Suddenly a watery being rises up out of the turbulent pool. Will you draw your weapon (turn to **33**), or find some other way to fight it (turn to **142**)?

115

Just ahead of you, draped over the gnarled branches of a tree, are several strands of long black hair. Could they be hair from a nun's head? You may:

Open your backpack	Turn to **158**
Go over to the tree	Turn to **34**
Ignore this and walk on	Turn to **221**

116

The Undine's power drains the very soul of its victims. As the last of your PSI passes away, you are cast into oblivion. Your lifeless body drops to the wet floor and is engulfed by the watery monster. Your adventure ends in annihilation.

117

Hopefully you will have more luck elsewhere. You may approach the adventurers (turn to **176**), the gypsies (turn to **56**) or even the innkeeper (turn to **227**). You glance at the horse brass again; if it occurs to you to try stealing it, turn to **190**.

118

You see a young couple outside the beer tent: a swarthy gypsy lad and his plump country maid. You ask where you could find someone with a crystal ball, and without looking away from the eyes of his paramour the lad replies, 'You want Gypsy Gayl. She's the best fortune teller for twenty leagues and more.' He points towards her caravan. Turn to **12**.

119

The curse takes its effect on you: in future you must reduce all your Combat Rolls by 1. For example, if you rolled a 7 in combat then you would actually count this as 6. You utter a stream of colourful invective at the fortune teller as you make good your escape with the purloined ball. Turn to **208**.

As you take the torch from the bracket, you set off
a trap! A hatch you had carelessly failed to notice
opens beneath you and you plummet some two
metres on to a cold stone floor. Somewhat dazed,
though remarkably unscathed, you stagger to your
feet and look around. In the bleary light and
choking dust you can just make out a shadowy
figure chained to the wall. As you approach with
the torch you see he is an old man with a clouded,
sightless right eye.

'I am Luther Faze,' he tells you. 'Are you the
champion my sons have sent to rescue me? If so,
help me out of these chains and your reward will
exceed anything you can imagine.'

If you wish to do as he asks, turn to **307**. If you
would rather leave him chained up, turn to **277**.

You are wandering in a limitless maze whose walls
are force-fields that reflect all light. At last you
reach a crossroads and try to decide where to go
from here.

To head north	Turn to **170**
To head south	Turn to **107**
To head east	Turn to **43**
To head west	Turn to **4**

Hushed, whispering voices seem to call from outside the tower – '*Awake, master. Death cannot hold you.*' You go to the window and look out, but there is nothing but the night and the howling wind.

Something stirs behind you. You freeze at the sound, then slowly turn . . . Slank has risen again, but altered now to his true form – he is much smaller than before, stooped, almost frail. His face is grey and lined, twisted and misshapen such that the hollow sockets of his eyes are not level. The effect is somehow even more horrible than his previous appearance.

'I still have one life left,' he snarls. The voice is a strangled, halting croak. His power is greatly diminished, but you will have to fight hard to prevail against him.

SLANK   VIGOUR **12**

Roll two dice:

score 2 to 6   You are wounded and lose 3 VIGOUR

score 7 to 12   The demon loses 3 VIGOUR

If you beat him, turn to **80**.

If you were bitten by the Giant Cobra, turn to **250**. If you have come through the fight unscathed, turn to **304**.

You hear some traders talking about a fete that is being held on the other side of town. You make your way there, thinking that perhaps you will meet someone who knows where you can get a crystal ball. You pass through the south gate of the town and almost at once find yourself in a milling throng of townsfolk and gypsies. Nearby, a group of people have gathered in a ring. They are shouting and cheering, and you stop to see what all the noise is about. There is a tall thin man with a scarlet bandanna around his head accepting coins from the people around him. He is taking bets on the outcome of a cock fight.

If you wish to place a bet yourself, turn to **77**.

If you decide to pass by, turn to **129**.

125

t occurs to you that you could try to heat the knife using your lantern, which might help it to

through the ice. If you want to do that, turn to **20**.
If you have a jar of salt, turn to **83**.

126

Will you leave the circular room through the door
to your left (turn to **240**), or will you return to the
landing and open the door with the copper plaque
(turn to **279**) or the door with the bronze plaque
(turn to **300**)?

127

The moment you lift the lid of the chest, a heavy
iron portcullis slides down across the open archway. If you had not dragged the chest out of
the room before opening it, you would now be
imprisoned. The chest contains nothing, but you
are too thankful to be disgruntled at this. Shudder-
ing at the fate you nearly suffered, you continue
on your way. Turn to **251**.

128

Sweat trickles into your eyes as the relentless battle
continues.

Roll two dice:
score 2 to 4	You are hit twice and lose 6 VIGOUR
score 5 to 6	You are hit once and lose 3 VIGOUR

score 7 to 12   One of the remaining robbers
                loses 3 VIGOUR

If you FLEE, turn to **219**. If you continue the fight
and beat another of them, turn to **59**.

129

You are jostled by a crowd of excited townsfolk. A
man in a long violet robe catches your eye. He has
been performing conjuring tricks – to the obvious
delight of his audience, who are clapping and
throwing silver coins. As you watch, he brushes
his fingers together and creates a flare of light and
a puff of green smoke. If you decide to pass by,
turn to **140**. If you want to wait and buy one of
the magical charms he has for sale, turn to **68**.

130

The shimmering passages meet at yet another
crossroads. Now, perhaps guided by a sixth sense,
you are almost sure which way you should go.
Will it be:

North?	Turn to **271**
South?	Turn to **64**
East?	Turn to **179**
West?	Turn to **121**

131

They call for more wine. It is obvious that they

want to get you drunk, but you are not so easily taken in. You politely tell them you have business elsewhere, and they shrug as you get up from the table. If you wish to chat to the innkeeper, turn to **227**. If you wish to make an attempt at pilfering the clover-leaf horse brass, turn to **190**.

132

About mid-morning you are passing between two hills when you come face-to-face with a Mountain Lion. It makes no immediate move to attack. You recover from an instant of petrifaction and consider your next action. Will you:

Draw your sword and fight it?	Turn to **22**
Climb the cliff out of its reach?	Turn to **67**
Wait to see what it does?	Turn to **229**

133

That's right!' he says, his tone of surprise veiling slight irritation. 'I didn't expect you to get that one. All the same, I don't see how you could have cheated, so I suppose I'll have to let you go for now . . .' Suddenly he spits in your face! You blink and rub your eyes, and when you look again he is nowhere to be seen. You go back to the top of the stairs and try the other direction. Turn to **7**.

134

You pause a few metres beyond the library, beside the other door. If you wish to open it, turn to **264**. If you wish to continue on along the corridor, turn to **135**.

135

After a short distance the corridor turns to the right. At the corner there is a low, fire-blackened door with a pewter handle. If you wish to examine the room beyond this door, turn to **48**. If you wish to ignore it and carry on, turn to **192**.

136

You hear a spring break inside the strange warrior and it abruptly sags down into the recess below the trapdoor. It now looks as harmless as a broken toy, but you see no point in waiting around to make sure of this. Slamming the trapdoor shut you make your way along the gallery. Turn to **308**.

137

Do you have the ashes of a saint? If so, you scatter these over the demon's body – turn to **309**.

If you don't have these, turn to **122**.

138

You could try heading for the castle by an indirect route – either to the right or left of where it actually seems to be (turn to **55**). You could try closing your eyes and heading on blindly in the direction you last saw it (turn to **9**). Or you could use an item from your backpack (turn to **62**).

139

You leave the newt's eye in the eyeslit of the demon mask. There seems to be nothing else you can do here, so you cross the icy floor to the archway and step through. Turn to **288**.

140

A short fat man blunders carelessly into you as he emerges from behind a caravan. He murmurs an indistinct apology as he brushes past. Roll one die. If you roll a 4 or better then you have your wits about you – turn to **109**. On a roll of 1–3, your attention is elsewhere – turn to **193**.

141

You scramble down under the arch of the bridge and search through the dead man's belongings. You get sixteen Gold Pieces and a magical Potion of Dazzling Speed. You may drink this at the *start* of any one combat; it will enable you to add 1 to your dice rolls *for that combat only*. You climb back up on to the bridge. As you are about to roll the Toll Collector's body into the river, you notice a jade horn-shaped amulet around his neck. You may take this if you wish – remember to note it on your Character Sheet, along with the other items. After disposing of the body you press on. Turn to **6**.

142

Which of the following will you use against the Undine?

The Ring of Light	Turn to **266**
The Potion of Dazzling Speed	Turn to **305**
Your lantern	Turn to **85**

If you decide not to try any of these, turn to **33**.

143

You rush forward with a snarl, but he ducks under your swing and responds with a powerful sword-thrust which you barely deflect in time. He jumps and weaves with confusing speed, and you soon see that he will be a difficult foe to beat.

TOLL COLLECTOR   VIGOUR 12

Roll two dice:
score 2 to 7   His blade cuts you; lose 3
                 VIGOUR

score 8 to 12   He loses 3 VIGOUR

If you win, turn to **141**.

144

The shrine consists simply of a marble dome supported by three thick pillars. Within, on a table of rock, you can see a verdigris-stained urn. As you step between the pillars a silvery light appears out of nowhere and haloes the urn. If you wish to stay, turn to **82**. You can of course flee from the spot and continue on towards the hills, in which case turn to **301**.

(illustration on previous page)

145

You look around the taproom, now strewn with the wreckage and gore of your battle. The third man, whom you noticed earlier, is cowering behind an overturned table. You stare into his eyes and draw your finger across your throat in a significant gesture. White as a sheet, he controls his trembling long enough to nod in understanding. You hurry away from The Four Leaf Clover with the stolen horse brass in your pocket. Turn to **273**.

146

You make your way up to the hut and rap smartly on the door. A small flap opens and a bloodshot eye peers out at you. You hear bolts being drawn back and the door is opened by a heavyset man in red and black robes. Seeing you, he smiles and holds up the jug of wine he has in one hand. 'As the sun sinks in its own blood and night strokes the land with fingers of shadow, let us drink together and pass merry comment on the transience of life!' It is obvious he has imbibed several jugs of wine already, as he seems to be slurring his words somewhat. If you wish to accept his offer, turn to **285**. Or will you leave, preferring to camp outside for the night – turn to **296**?

147

Each door bears a plaque with an inscription on it, and these read as follows:

Copper plaque – *To slay me you must pass through this door.*

Bronze plaque – *You should not pass through this door.*

Lead plaque – *The correct path is not beyond the copper-plaque door.*

You grit your teeth. Slank is obviously toying with you. His mistake. You may open one of the doors – the door with the copper plaque (turn to **279**), the one with the bronze plaque (turn to **300**) or the one with the lead plaque (turn to **101**). Or you may take an item from your backpack, in which case turn to **200**.

You have no hope of success without a sword to fight with. You stop off at a weaponsmith's shop on your way to the town gate. The weaponsmith looks up from his work as you enter. He is an old fellow with an affable grin. 'Aha,' he cries. 'My first customer of the day. Come in, come in.' You tell him what you require and he replies that he will charge you fifteen Gold Pieces, but that the sword you buy will be the finest that any craftsman could produce. You pay him (he accepts one dose of the rare Salve of Healing in lieu of payment, if you have no cash) and take the sword. The workmanship of the blade is indeed excellent, and you thank the old weaponsmith as he helps you fix the scabbard to your belt.

Glad to have a sword at your side once more, you hurry on through the streets and soon reach the western gate. Turn to 72.

You step back from the door as Garl's ponderous footsteps approach. You watch as the latch is slowly raised. The door swings open and Garl stands there axe in hand, blinking as his eyes become accustomed to the darkness. With a yell you swing your sword in a surprise attack. Garl grunts as the blade bites into his flesh. As he bares his teeth you suddenly know him for what he is – not a man at all, but an evil Ogre!

OGRE   VIGOUR 12

Roll two dice:
score 2 to 6   You are hit; lose 4 VIGOUR
score 7 to 12   The Ogre loses 3 VIGOUR

Note that because of his great strength he can deal terrible wounds with his axe. If you beat him, turn to **281**.

150

He shrugs and seems to fade away into the shadows. You are alone in the dungeon. Turn to **277**.

151

'ou take the rod from him and soon find that you
re barely able to hold on to it – the fish is putting

up quite a struggle. Shortly the big man returns with a net and takes hold of the rod. With a mighty effort he draws up a spined vicious-looking fish the size of a dog. 'Quite a whopper!' says the man, showing a set of sharp white teeth as he grins. 'How rare to find a person in these days of selfishness and antagonism who is prepared to lend a hand to a fellow creature!' He takes a ring from his finger. 'Allow me to offer my Ring of Light as a gift for your assistance. Moreover, as a special favour to you, today I shall dine on fish.'

You are not quite sure what he means by this last remark, but you accept the magic ring and than him before going on your way. Turn to **132**.

152

Hrothgar lives in a rambling house close to the town centre. He opens the door to you himself – a small thin man with a ginger beard. He gets few visitors, and invites you in at once when he hears your story, that you are a collector and connoisseur of antique armour. He shows you his small but valuable collection, including the suit of plate worn by the pure and valiant knight of legend, Sir Quedrey. While the trusting Hrothgar fetches tea and cakes, you quickly shave a fragment from the armour's epauliére with the edge of your dagger. He will never notice its loss. You enjoy his hospitality for a while longer and then make your excuses and leave. Turn to **269**.

As you step through the open doorway, your lantern gutters and dies. Before being plunged into darkness, you had a momentary impression of standing in the hall of gleaming mirrors. Suddenly you are falling! You reach out in panic, flailing desperately for some handhold, but you are surrounded by emptiness. Knowing that the impact will be worse if your muscles are tense, you force your body to relax. You crash to the floor with a sickening thud, but luckily you are only stunned. After a few moments you sit up and feel around for your lantern. As you rekindle it, you see that you are at the junction of four passages. The walls are flickering planes of reflective force. You try to decide which way to go, but all directions look the same. You could head north (turn to **170**), south (turn to **107**), east (turn to **43**) or west (turn to **4**).

Naturally!' replies the tallest gypsy with a grin. After finishing their wine, they take you to the fete just outside the town, where they point out Gypsy Gayl's caravan. You approach it eagerly, praying that here you will find a crystal ball for your quest. Turn to **12**.

155

'Know where you can find some,' one of them replies. 'If you'll pay us, say, five Gold Pieces for our trouble, we'll take you there right now.' They drain their tankards and sit back, waiting for your answer. Will you agree to go with them (turn to **286**), or ask if they know where you can get a crystal ball as well (turn to **224**)? You could refuse to pay what they ask, of course. If so, will you strike up a conversation with the innkeeper (turn to **227**), or try to steal the clover-shaped brass that hangs over the bar (turn to **190**)?

156

You haul the grating aside and stare down into the pit. The walls are smooth, and slimy with an eerie grey lichen. A gaunt man wearing a jewelled eyepatch stands at the bottom. 'Saved! Saved at last!' he cries, waving to you. 'Throw me the rope, won't you?' If you wish to lower the rope down to him, turn to **302**. If you prefer to leave to head along the corridor, turn to **2**.

157

'Oh, we don't grow that,' one of them replies. 'It gives th' cows wind!' They all laugh uproariously. Another adds, 'Maybe we'd know better if we 'ad another drink inside us.' They peer significantly into their now-empty tankards. Will you buy them

more drinks, at a cost of three Gold Pieces (turn to
213), or will you take your leave of them (turn to
117)?

158

As you open your backpack, a thick bank of fog
engulfs you, obscuring your vision for a moment.
When you look into the pack, you discover that
the items you collected to deal with the demon
have gone! You crouch dejectedly by your open
backpack. What will you do now – go back and
tell Jasper that the mists stole your items (turn to
90), or walk on (turn to **30**)?

159

You ask the genie for a clue to defeating Slank.
'The eyes have it,' he replies cryptically. 'I suggest
you go back to the landing and try a different
door, o bountiful one!' With a sudden glare of
light, he disappears. Turn to **126**.

160

You leave the teardrop in the mask's one eye
and then cross the room to the archway. Before
continuing, remember to cross the tear off your
Character Sheet. Now turn to **288**.

You strike one of them down. Momentarily the others edge back, and you have the opportunity to FLEE out into the street if you wish. If you take this escape route, turn to **37** – but if you fail the AGILITY roll for FLEEING you will suffer three wounds (for a total of 12 VIGOUR points).

If you choose to fight on, turn to **57** if and when you defeat another of them.

Roll two dice:

score 2	You are hit three times and lose 12 VIGOUR
score 3 to 4	You are hit twice; lose 6 VIGOUR
score 5 to 6	You are hit once and lose 3 VIGOUR
score 7 to 12	One of your opponents (you choose which) loses 3 VIGOUR

162

She glances whimsically into her crystal ball and instantly perceives your intention of acquiring it. 'Foolish thief!' she snarls. With a snap of her fingers she summons two burly gypsies who brandish wide-bladed knives. You cannot get to the doorway. This is a fight to the death.

First GYPSY   VIGOUR 12

Roll two dice:

score 2 to 6   You are wounded and lose 3
                 VIGOUR
score 7 to 12   The Gypsy loses 3 VIGOUR

In the cramped caravan, they do not have space to come at you together. If you beat this one, turn to **75**.

163

You double up in sudden and intense agony as you clench your teeth around a stifled scream. For long minutes you crouch there by the fire, incapacitated by the terrible pain. At last you are able to rise, but you have *permanently* lost a point of VIGOUR. Reduce your *normal* VIGOUR by 1. You can now either open the larder (turn to **63**) or go through to the next room (turn to **240**).

164

You return to the inn early the next day. Looking around the taproom, you see only a few customers drinking alone. The gypsies are not here. The innkeeper grunts as you bid him good morning. If you wish to question him, turn to **227**. If you would rather try to steal the clover horse brass, turn to **190**.

165

You struggle to move, to turn and run before it is too late, but your muscles are locked rigid by the Cobra's hypnosis. Still weaving its head in the entrancing rhythm, it advances towards you. Horror-struck, you have no choice but to watch as it readies itself for the final, fatal strike. Then its poison-flecked fangs snap forward, and your adventure ends in instant death.

166

He comes over and lays his hands on your shoulders – apparently in a gesture of friendship, but you feel as if you are bound in shackles of cold iron. He fixes you with his one good eye and says, 'I have a riddle for you. My first is equality, my last is inferiority, and my whole is superiority – what am I?' Decide on your answer (think carefully!) and then turn to **196**.

167

'You're being remarkably unhelpful,' says the lion coolly. 'I mean to say, why do you humans have to be so preposterously timid anyway?' It walks off as proudly as its limp will allow. After some time you decide that it is safe to lower yourself to the ground and go on. Turn to **24**.

168

The door swings ponderously open into a cavernous crypt. The sound of dripping water echoes in the stillness and you see that the walls and pillars are encrusted with uneven lumps of damp limestone. You swing the light of the lantern around and your attention is caught by a massive sarcophagus at the far side of the crypt. Will you:

Investigate the sarcophagus?	Turn to **203**
Cross to an archway in the opposite wall?	Turn to **234**
Return to the passage and continue the way you were going?	Turn to **44**

169

Following instructions in his book, Luther affixes the sliver of armour to the point of one of your arrows. He then restrings your bow using the nun's hair. 'This will kill Slank at once if you shoot him through the heart,' he explains. 'Lastly, then, do you have the ashes of a saint?'

If you do, turn to **275**. If not, turn to **88**.

170

You reach a point where four identical passages meet. Which way will you go from here:

North?	Turn to **51**
South?	Turn to **64**
East?	Turn to **179**
West?	Turn to **249**

171

You wake up in a gutter about midnight. Wincing at your terrible hangover, you slowly get to your feet. You have vague recollections of ordering several bottles of wine, but the gypsies quickly got you drunk and everything else is a blank. With sudden alarm, you reach for your money pouch. Gone! They looted all your cash. Turn to **164**.

172

Slank can scent your fear and almost hear your racing heartbeat – although blind, he is yet dangerous. He lunges at you with the long, sparkling talons of his right hand, using them as a fencer uses a sword.

SLANK   VIGOUR **24**

Roll two dice:
score 2 to 6   You are struck; lose 3 VIGOUR
score 7 to 12   The demon loses 3 VIGOUR

If you win, turn to **137**.

'Awfully decent of you,' says the lion as you draw
the thorn from its paw. 'Rather embarrassing really
– can't think how I came to tread on the damned
thing! If you're heading west, let me give you
some advice. There are two tribes of goblins in
these hills, the Drans and the Kabbagoos. You can
never tell the difference between them because
they mix freely and wear the same outlandish
clothes. The only thing is that the Drans always
tell the truth and the Kabbagoos always lie. I hope
that's of some help to you.' After thanking you
again, the lion goes on its way. You consider what
it has told you as you head further west. Turn to
24.

You drop your sword and ask for quarter. 'Base
varlet!' cries the knight, shaking with rage. 'I
should spit you like a pig where you stand – but
nay, for you have requested mercy, and I would
not slay an unarmed foe. Begone!'

You scurry off through the crowds, head bowed
in disgrace. Not only have you failed to steal the
knight's helmet, but you have lost your trusty
sword. Unless you have the money to buy another
(which will cost fifteen Gold Pieces) you must
fight with your dagger from now on; this means
that you must subtract 1 from all your future
Combat Rolls.

Your sole option now is to get the armour fragment you seek from the collection of Hrothgar the scholar. Turn to **152**.

175

Only one of the treacherous adventurers still lives. He had intended to rob you, but now he is fighting for his life.

Roll two dice:
score 2 to 4   You are hit; lose 3 VIGOUR
score 5 to 12   The adventurer loses 3 VIGOUR

If you kill him, turn to **105**. There is now room for you to get past him and FLEE back along the path to town; if you do this, turn to **287**.

176

You buy a round of drinks (deduct four Gold Pieces) and go over to their table. Obviously new travels quickly in this town, because one of them nods as you introduce yourself and says, 'Ah, you're the one who got the Faze contract, aren't you?'

Will you ask them if they know where you can get a crystal ball (turn to **278**), or do you start by mentioning a four leaf clover (turn to **155**)?

177

'Ho there!' he cries, struggling with the fishing rod. 'A fine one has taken the bait this morning, but I need a net before I land him. Will you hold the rod a few minutes while I fetch one from my cottage?

Will you do as he asks (turn to **151**), or decline and go on your way (turn to **132**)?

178

You hold forth the ring and cause it to emit a brilliant flare. The Marshons clutch at their huge eyes and fall back whimpering, blinded by the light. They scurry off into the safety of the darkness. Turn to **66**.

179

You are lost in an infinite network of passages. The walls are perfectly smooth mirrors – probably planes of magical force, for you cannot mark them in any way. Arriving at a junction, will you go:

North?   Turn to **170**
South?   Turn to **107**
East?   Turn to **43**
West?   Turn to **4**

180

You pound the door with your fist, producing a booming echo. After a few moments a small panel slides back and the occupant of the room examines you. You see his eyes alight on the talisman Jasper gave you; immediately he gives a cry of delight and starts to clear his barricade from the other side of the door. You wait nervously in the passage, praying that all this noise won't alert the demon. Finally the door opens and the old man ushers you in. The place is a vast, vaulted library with all manner of books and pamphlets lining every inch of the walls from floor to ceiling.

'You've come at last!' says the old man, crying with joy. 'I knew my lads wouldn't let me down – I'm Luther Faze, of course.' He shows you to a leather armchair by the fireplace and thrusts a glass of tawny port wine into your hand. Obviously although Slank's prisoner, he is not completely without creature comforts. He takes down a must tome and opens it at a chapter headed *Dealing with Demons*. 'Now listen carefully, for there isn't much time. You should have a number of items and this book describes how each item will affect Slank. Firstly, a four leaf clover will have much the same effect on him as a crucifix has on

vampire – he won't want to touch it or go anywhere near it. Second, if you throw my daughter's
teardrop into his left eye you'll blind him completely, as I've already managed to destroy his
right eye. Now, do you have the fragment of
knight's armour and the hair of a nun?'

If you have both these items turn to **169**. If not,
turn to **10**.

181

You can use one of the following items, if you
have them:

The four leaf clover	Turn to **104**
The daughter's teardrop	Turn to **160**
A newt's eye	Turn to **139**

If you do not have any of these, or do not wish to
use them, you now leave the room (turn to **288**).

182

If you are wounded, he restores your VIGOUR to
its *normal* score. If you are unwounded, he magi
cally increases your *normal* VIGOUR by 1 point
You are about to see if you can get another wish
out of him when you notice that you are alone in
the room. Turn to **126**.

183

You get a whiff of the stuff in the cauldron whe

you are only halfway across the room, and it almost puts you off taking a look. When you do look, you wish you hadn't – it is a green, slimy broth full of unmentionable ingredients. If by any chance you want to drink this foul brew, turn to **53**. Otherwise you could continue on into the next room (turn to **240**) or investigate the larder (turn to **63**).

184

You are spotted and there are shouts of anger. Four of the robbers start to run back along the road towards you. They are zigzagging so as to present difficult targets – and you feel your marksmanship is somewhat below par today in any case. You draw your sword and close with them.

UKNOR the Barbarian	VIGOUR 12
JORKISS the Sly	VIGOUR 6
Crazy NIAL	VIGOUR 9
BOSO HEADCUT	VIGOUR 9

Roll two dice:

score 2	You are struck four times; lose 12 VIGOUR
score 3 to 4	You are struck three times; lose 9 VIGOUR
score 5 to 6	You are struck twice; lose 6 VIGOUR
score 7 to 8	You are struck a single blow; lose 3 VIGOUR

score 9 to 12   One of the robbers (you choose
                  which) loses 3 VIGOUR

If you FLEE, remember that all four will strike at
you as you turn to run – you must suffer the loss
of 12 VIGOUR points if you fail the AGILITY roll.
If you do this, turn to **219**. If you fight and manage
to kill one, turn to **28**.

185

He is only too glad to be able to assist you in your
noble undertaking. He holds out his gauntlet for
you to take, but you point out that you need only
a small fragment. Swiftly he shaves a sliver from
his helmet with the sharp edge of his sword. Turn
to **269**.

186

You take hold of one of the iron rings fixed into
the chest and manage to haul it across the floor of
the chamber. The shadows cluster less thickly in
the passage. Lifting your lantern, you play its
beam across the chest. The metal hasp is carved to
resemble a lidless eye. You may open the chest
(turn to **127**), or leave it where it is and continue
your exploration of the castle (turn to **251**).

187

After a brief uneasy glance at the bas relief, you

step through the arch and make your way along a narrow twisting passage that leads deep into the heart of the castle. You pass through a succession of gloomy chambers and finally climb a worn flight of steps to a landing where three doors face you. Turn to **147**.

188

After two hours or so you are on the verge of nodding off when a slight noise jerks you to full wakefulness. You creep over to the bedroom door and peer through the keyhole. Garl is moving around laying the table for a meal. After putting out a fork and a long sharp knife, he brings a large metal tub from the kitchen and places this beside your door. You realize he is about to listen at the keyhole, so you pretend to snore. He turns away. Peering out again, you see he is taking a huge axe from the cupboard. Will you gather your things and make a getaway via the bedroom window (turn to **76**), or draw your sword and get ready to fight him if he comes in (turn to **149**)?

189

You leave the road and sneak around through the trees, giving the commotion a wide berth. When you are safely past, you resume your journey into the hills. Turn to **92**.

190

You stroll casually up to the bar and order a drink. When the innkeeper turns away to pour it, you surreptitiously reach up for the horse brass. Roll one die. If you score a 1 or 2, turn to **259**. If you score a 3 or higher, turn to **110**.

191

On a plinth in front of the idol – which depicts the god Lurgai during his thirty-seventh Tribulation – you find a vase containing fresh flowers. You should note these down on your Character Sheet if you decide to take them. Will you now:

Carry on towards the Mungo Hills?	Turn to **301**
Place an offering of gold before the idol?	Turn to **212**
Investigate further?	Turn to **239**

192

You go only a short distance before arriving at a door. On the floor in front of you, eight crimson-fletched arrows have been placed in an intriguing pattern. You may pick up the arrows if you wish; remember to note them on your Character Sheet if so. There is no other way on from here, so you step forward and open the door. Turn to **153**.

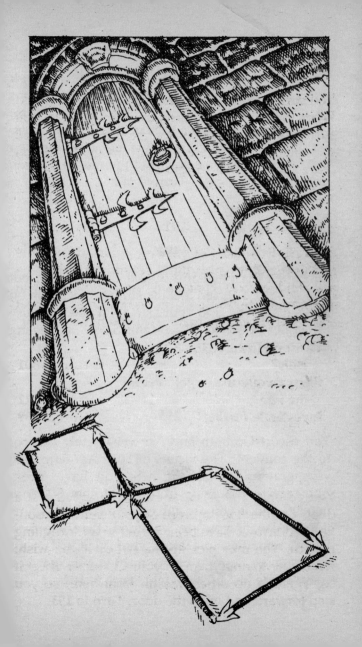

193

You go on for a short distance, then (belatedly) it strikes you that there was something suspicious about the fat man. If you bought a Luck Charm, you find you no longer have it. If you did not buy a Charm, you notice that the money pouch on your belt has been stolen, and the thief has made off with all your cash. Turn to **118**.

194

You open the phial and tip out the teardrop, but to no effect. You can feel the stinging secretion on the walls eating into your skin. Will you now use the ashes (turn to **98**), or the Salve of Healing (turn to **267**)?

195

You escort Gorbran and Norwena safely on foot to the convent. The Sisters of Pure Adoration are very grateful for all the help you have given. You receive a blessing from the Mother Superior herself, and if you are subject to a curse it is now lifted. Also, if you are wounded, they use their herbal remedies to restore your VIGOUR to its *normal* score. After a hearty meal you are given a comfortable bed for the night. Turn to **102**.

The correct answer is 'peerless'. If you answered this, turn to **133**. If you answered anything else, turn to **235**.

Again you find yourself at a nexus from which four mirrored passageways lead off. From here you may head:

North	Turn to **170**
South	Turn to **107**
East	Turn to **43**
West	Turn to **130**

You level your bow and loose five arrows in rapid succession. Roll one die for each arrow. On a roll of 3 or better it finds its target, but on a roll of 1 or 2 it misses. If at least three arrows hit, turn to **233**. If you miss with more than two, however, turn to **184**.

You enter a large, low-ceilinged room with no other doorways. In the centre of the room stands a tall man in voluminous robes. He wears a patch over his right eye and stands by a pool of blood which is flowing from a gash in his arm. If you want to talk to him, turn to **166**. If you want to take an item from your backpack, turn to **201**.

- 200

You can use the crystal ball (turn to **272**) or the three strange silver coins (turn to **5**). If you have neither of these, or decide not to use them, turn back to **147** and open one of the doors.

201

Your eyes are off him for only a moment as you reach for your backpack, but when you look again he is no longer there. Strange and inexplicable things are obviously commonplace in Slank's castle – you will have to be on your guard from now on. You turn back and go the other way; turn to **27**.

You proceed along the trail, hoping that you have made the correct choice and that you will soon be in the swamps of Bosh. Just then, a rumbling comes from below your feet. The ground shakes and great fissures and cracks appear across the path. You fall and are engulfed by scalding steam that issues out of the depths of the earth. You cannot see, and when you try to cry out the steam sears your throat. You have taken the trail leading to Dragonbreath Canyon, but you will never live to reach that terrible place. Your adventure ends here.

Etched into the crumbling marble lid of the sarcophagus are the outlines of a stern cruel-lipped face. From the crown across its brow, you determine that this is the coffin of a prince. You could lift the lid – in which case, turn to **19** – but an inner voice seems to counsel against it. If you decide to leave the crypt, will you go on through the archway (turn to **234**) or return to the passage you have come from (turn to **44**).

Smiling viciously, Slank steps from the alcove and towers over you in his robes as black as the night. At first glance his face might almost be considered

handsome – but then you see the clouded, sightless right eye, the face around it scarred and mutilated by terrible burns. The other eye shines with an awful, corrupt light, and the expression twisting those fine features is one of utter and inhuman evil. From outside the tower comes the rumble of distant thunder, and Slank answers it with triumphant laughter.

If you have Elvira Faze's teardrop, you can cast it into his eye – turn to **303**. If you don't have this item, you must fight him – turn to **257**.

205

Do you have a sword? If so, turn to **72**. If you lost your sword earlier, turn to **148**.

206

Slank is trying to convince you to serve him. You dimly realize that he is probably using magic, but you cannot resist. The force of his will swamps yours. He steps from the alcove and you find yourself kneeling before him. Now and forever, you are his cringing thrall . . .

207

You have a horrible notion that the sword is going to fall and impale you as you step beneath it. For once, your suspicions are unfounded. Leaving the sword dangling behind you, you head along the corridor. Turn to **113**.

208

You now have the crystal ball you needed. Make sure you have noted it down on your Character Sheet. Do you have the four leaf clover as well? If not, turn to **256**. If you have this item, turn to **273**.

209

One of the gypsies grins, showing uneven white teeth. 'Why not ask the innkeeper?' he suggests. You go over to the bar and ask the innkeeper if he knows where you can get the clover you need. Turn to **227**.

210

The instant you strike the first spark from your flint, the Mashons rush forward eagerly towards the source of light. You are engulfed by hundreds of slippery, clambering bodies. More and more Marshons surge into the struggling horde, anxious to see the light, and you are soon crushed by the stampede. Your adventure ends here.

211

Before continuing on your way, you could take either the poleaxe or the now-lifeless rug. You cannot take both because they are rather bulky items. If you wish to take one, remember to note it on your Character Sheet. You procede to the double doors at the end of the room. Turn to **276**.

212

Placing a single coin on the plinth before the idol, you utter a short prayer to Lurgai in which you compare your current adventure to his ninth Tribulation. There is no immediate response from the god. Will you now carry on towards the hills (turn to **301**), or look around for a while (turn to **239**)?

213

To your dismay – if not utter surprise – they lapse into a drunken rambling and then fall asleep. Annoyed at wasting your money, you mutter an oath and get up from the table. Turn to **117**.

214

Searching in the darkness, your fingers find the hasp of the chest. You flip it open and lift the lid. As you do, there is a screech of metal and a brutal clang from the direction of the archway. You spin around to discover that your exit from the room is now blocked by a stout iron portcullis. You rush over and seize the bars, but it is obvious that you would need superhuman strength to bend them.

If you have a Potion of Strength in your backpack, you can drink it now and escape (turn to **251**). If you do not have this item you are hopelessly trapped, and now you can only wait for a lingering death by starvation or else draw your weapon and die by your own hand . . .

215

With his magic, he adds 1 point to your *normal* AGILITY score. You are about to thank him when you notice that he has vanished. Turn to **126**.

216

An emerald vapour issues from the open neck of the bottle. When it clears you discover a tall figure with green skin standing before you. Arms folded across his barrel-like chest, he bows low. 'Greetings, esteemed one!' he booms. 'I am Rashid al-Adir, and for releasing me I can grant you a boon of skill, stamina or knowledge.'

Which will you choose? If skill, turn to **215**. If stamina, turn to **182**. If knowledge, turn to **159**.

217

The trail takes you down out of the hills. Ahead of you the horizon is lost in a blur of mist. Realizing that it will be difficult to find dry wood with which to start a campfire in the dank swamp land, you gather kindling as you descend the trail

When you reach the low lying moors and marshes of Bosh you progress is slowed considerably, for you have to make your way around tracts of treacherous mire. The tendrils of mist are like fingers groping round the silhouetted shapes of bent and deformed trees. Out of the corner of your eye you catch sight of something – a crystal ball, just off the path to your left! It looks unsettlingly like the one you should have in your backpack. Will you go over to the crystal ball to examine it (turn to **262**), check that the original ball is still in your backpack (turn to **158**), or simply walk on (turn to **115**)?

218

You are only a few yards from the archway, but the terrible cold numbs your limbs and you slump down on the icy floor. You cannot feel any pain, but you realize you are dying. You note with dispassionate wonder the curious sighing sound your breath makes as it freezes on the air. Strangely calm, you surrender to the eternal dark . . .

219

They pursue you for a little way along the road, but soon give up the chase and go back to loot their victims. You press on briskly towards the setting sun, determined to put several miles between you and the robbers before making camp. Turn to **92**.

220

Beyond the door you find a confusing network of winding tunnels. You stride along them, trusting your sixth sense to take you to the demon's lair. As you pass through a lofty shadow-filled hall, a peal of shrieking laughter comes echoing to you from a distant part of the castle. You have the horrible feeling that your every move is being watched. Ahead of you, worn steps spiral upwards and you climb them to a landing where three doors face you. Turn to **147**.

221

The mist's fingers poke and pry, stroke and search, around your backpack. You realize that the mist itself is like an entity – a wraith which creates illusions to try and trick you. You are not fooled. Turn to **60**.

222

You continue on through the bleak scenery of Bosh for some time, but you still do not seem to be able to get any closer to your objective. Perhaps the crystal ball will prove of use now? You take it from your backpack. Turn to **242**.

223

Seeing you defeat four skilled opponents single-handed, the remaining robbers turn tail and run. Your dashing rescue came just in time for the damsel who now steps down from the coach. Her expression registers a momentary disapproval at your bloodied and travel-soiled appearance. Then she smiles and thanks you for intervening. The old man, who has been cringing under the coach, now realizes that the robbers have gone. He crawls out, dusts himself off and retrieves his staff. You glance at the guard who was so valiantly fighting on to protect these two, but you see that he has been cut down while you were battling the four robbers. The old man explains that he is Gorbran, a servant of the Sisters of Pure Adoration. He was escorting the damsel, whose name is Norwena, back to the convent where she is to be initiated into the Holy Order. Since they now lack guards for their journey, you agree to accompany them. Turn to **195**.

224

They shrug. 'Can't help you there.' You finish your drink and ask them to take you to the clover. Turn to **286**.

225

A Luck Charm can be used *three times only*, so you must keep track of how often you use it. Any time you are required to make a dice roll (including a combat roll) you can activate the Charm instead. Using the Charm means that you do not need to roll the dice – you can proceed as if you had rolled whatever score you wanted. You must decide *in advance* when you use the Charm; you cannot use it to change the outcome of a dice roll after you have attempted and failed.

Remember that this item will work only three times, so use its powers wisely. Turn to **140**.

226

You feel a stab of excruciating pain as the snake's venom reaches your heart. Momentarily you fear for your life, but your robust constitution saves you. After a few minutes' rest you are strong enough to continue your adventure. Turn to **304**.

227

The innkeeper says that there are sometimes four

leaf clovers to be found in the beer garden at the back '. . . Hence the name of the inn!' he chuckles. You go out through the door he indicates and find yourself in the beer garden. Several elegantly dressed merchants are seated on a wooden bench. Their merriment turns to incredulity as they watch you get down on your hands and knees and start to peer at the lawn. After nearly an hour you are on the point of giving up when you spot what you are looking for; with a cry of triumph you pluck the four leaf clover. Note it down on your Character Sheet and turn to **124**.

228

You slice through her bonds with your knife and carry her over to a corner of the room where you gently set her down. The woman nurses her blistered feet for a while, then looks up at you and speaks. 'I was a witch, and I sold my soul to the demon in return for knowledge and occult power. For helping me, I will give you what little aid I can.' She puts a catskin pouch around your neck – increase your PSI score by 2 points (even above its *normal* level) for as long as you wear this. She also gives you three silver coins. 'These may show you the way,' she murmurs cryptically. You examine the coins and see that each has a unicorn's head on one face and a serpent's head with forked tongue on the other. You are about to question her further when you see that she has passed out. You moisten her lips with a little wine

then pocket the coins (remember to note them on your Character Sheet) and leave. Turn to **187**.

229

The lion holds up its paw to show you that there is a large thorn stuck right through it. Then, to your amazement, it speaks. 'Um, I seem to have this thorn . . .' You realize that the poor creature means you no harm, and resolve to help it. Turn to **173**.

230

With breathtaking speed and agility he leaps up and alights on the bridge in front of you. As he does so, he draws a long curved sword from the scabbard slung across his back. 'The fine for non payment of the toll is seven Gold Pieces,' he says with a wry smile. 'And the penalty for non payment of the *fine* is . . .' He glances meaningfully at the gleaming naked blade of his sword. Will you now pay him seven Gold Pieces (turn to **13**), or do you prefer to fight (turn to **143**)?

231

The Rauchwurm dissipates into the smoke from which it formed. You reach out and grasp the golden hilt of the sword you have fought to obtain. Certainly it is a worthy prize. As you swing through the air it follows your intentions with an almost sentient precision. When fighting with this enchanted weapon, you inflict extra damage on an enemy – every successful hit will cause your opponent to lose 4 VIGOUR points, rather than the usual 3 points. Seeing nothing else of value in the room, you turn to leave, again saved from electrocution by the power of your Wristband of Lightning. Turn to **192**.

232

The hole is damp, yet it is a great relief to be out of the icy bombardment. Above the thudding sounds of the hailstones outside you hear a soft squelching. To your horror, the surrounding 'walls' are closing in. A liquid oozes from them and trickles down around your feet. Your feet – as you look down, you see they are being sucked into what you took for mud. An odour like bile rises past you. You cannot escape. Your legs are trapped and you feel as though the strength is being drawn from you – as a morsel of food might feel in an enormous stomach, perhaps . . .

You have only moments in which to act. Desperately you search your backpack for something to use. Will you try:

The ashes of a saint?	Turn to **98**
The Salve of Healing?	Turn to **267**
The girl's teardrop?	Turn to **194**

A shower of arrows find their mark, throwing the robbers into confusion. They do not wait around long enough to see that it is a lone archer who attacks them. They break in a mad dash for the woods, and are soon lost from sight. You walk to the scene of the ambush. The guard has taken a mortal wound, and he looks up at you with dimming eyes. 'My thanks, stranger,' he gasps. 'Your rescue came just too late for me, I fear . . .' His breath rattles in his throat and he falls back.

An elegant velvet slipper emerges from the coach and you glance over as a slender damsel steps down. She surveys the carnage for a moment, then turns a pouting frown on the broken axle of the coach. The old man gets up from where he lay cowering in the dust and approaches you, drawing his dignity about him like a cloak. 'We are indebted to you,' he says haughtily. 'Had you not intervened when you did, things might have turned out for the worse. I am Gorbran, servant of the worshipful Sisters of Pure Adoration. This lady is Norwena, whom I am taking to join the convent.'

You are not one to ignore the gifts of providence. Pointing out that Gorbran and Norwena now lack guards for their journey, you appoint yourself their escort until they reach the convent. Turn to **195**.

Passing through a series of progressively more gloomy chambers, you finally come to a flight of worn stone steps that take you up to a narrow landing. Three doors face you. Turn to **147**.

Chuckling humourlessly, he closes his grip on you. You cannot move. 'Quite wrong,' he says. 'Clearly your riddling skills leave much to be desired, but perhaps they will improve when you've been a guest at my castle for an eternity or two!' By his duplicity, the archfiend Slank has captured you. You are his prisoner forever, and the adventure ends here.

He scratches the back of his neck. 'Don't know about the strand of hair,' he says after some thought – 'don't nuns shave their heads when they enter a convent, anyway? But there is a sort of shrine not too far from here where some old holy man was buried. Maybe he was a saint, who knows?' The toll collector gives you directions, and you set off in search of the shrine. Turn to **144**.

237

You check the little man's pockets and find several pilfered money pouches. His ill-gotten gains amount to 17 Gold Pieces. He also wears a cornelian ring in the shape of a skull, which you may take if you wish. Remember to note anything you take in the appropriate box on your Character Sheet. You find some grass to clean the blood from your sword, then step out from between the tents as if nothing had happened. Turn to **118**.

238

The Dwarf falls and a thin trickle of blood slowly runs down his chin into his matted beard. Having seen an earlier example of his cunning, you keep your weapon at his throat as you stoop to examine the body. In a pocket of his jerkin you find a watch on a chain. Dwarves are renowned for their skill at crafting clockwork devices, and the watch should fetch a good price – as long as you survive to sell it. Remember to note it down on your Character Sheet if you decide to keep it. Turning away from the stiffening little corpse, you head for the door at the end of the gallery. Turn to **220**.

239

It strikes you that if someone has left fresh flowers by the idol, there may be a religious community nearby. Perhaps you could get one or both of the

items you need? Roll one die. If you roll 4 or higher, turn to **244**. If you roll a 3 or less, turn to **260**.

240

You enter a long, oak-beamed dining hall with fading portraits high up on the walls. Ignoring two smaller doorways, you make your way along the table towards the double doors at the far end of the room. You pass a wide stone hearth where a raging log fire crackles and spits. Over the hearth hangs a great poleaxe and on the floor in front of it there is a fine, white bearskin rug. You can either go over to the hearth (turn to **290**) or carry on to the double doors (turn to **276**).

(illustration on previous page)

241

Holding up your lantern, you cross over to the archway – only to find that the passage beyond ends in a blank wall after only a few yards. You search in vain for a secret panel, but you are finally forced to accept that it is a dead end. Puzzled, you return to the hallway and try the stairs. Turn to **103**.

242

When you gaze at the castle through the crystal ball, a shimmering path of green light is visible leading through the swamp. Holding the crysta ball in front of your eyes, you make your way along the path. You have been walking for only a few minutes, intent on the ground where you tread, when you notice a dark shape looming ahead. You glance up from the crystal ball and almost drop it in shock. You are at the castle gates. Turn to **108**.

243

You reach into the silvery glow and take the urn. Peeking within, you see that it contains a handful of ashes. Somehow you know that these are the mortal remains of a saint. You put the urn in your backpack and set off again towards the hills. Turn to **301**.

244

You identify some tracks leading to the other side of the valley. Following these, you find your way to a shrine. Turn to **144**.

245

You have fallen victim to a spell of blood thinning. In future, at the end of any combat in which you are wounded you must roll one die. The number you roll will be the number of additional VIGOUR points you lose before you can staunch the bleeding. While you bemoan your ill luck, the detestable

Chonchon shrieks with laughter and flies off into the mists. Turn to **222**.

246

They are wary of you at first because you are from out of town, but when you buy them flagons of ale they soon become quite affable. Deduct three Gold Pieces for the drinks. You decide to ask if they know where you could get one of the items you need – will you enquire first about the crystal ball (turn to **87**) or the four leaf clover (turn to **157**)?

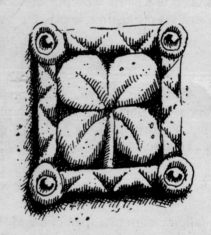

247

The cock you backed utters its last squawk. Yo

lose the money you wagered. The tall man is taking bets on another fight, but you decide to press on. Turn to **129**.

248

You stare with horrified eyes as the Cobra weaves closer. You want to run, but you cannot move a muscle. At the very last moment, just as it is about to strike, you shrug off the effects of its hypnosis and throw yourself back through the archway. The Cobra hisses at you, but makes no move to pursue as you hurry away along the passage. Turn to **251**.

249

You continue through the labyrinth of mirror-walled passages until you reach another cross-roads. From here, will you go:

North?	Turn to **170**
South?	Turn to **93**
East?	Turn to **43**
West?	Turn to **4**

250

Roll four dice (or roll one die four times). If the total exceeds your *current* VIGOUR score, turn to **94**. If not, turn to **226**.

251

Walking along the passage, you see a stone door in the wall to your left. If you wish to try the door, turn to **168**. If you wish to pass by, turn to **44**.

252

It is a fine morning and you enjoy your walk up into the rolling landscape of the Mungo Hills. After a little while you come to a stream where a burly man sits fishing. If you wish to greet him, turn to **177**. If you prefer to pass by, turn to **132**.

253

Hovering directly above your head, the fourth Chonchon glares down at its massacred comrades. *'Nemo me impune lacessit!'* it hisses. Obviously it is not wishing you well, for the next moment you feel a hostile spell closing around you. Try to roll equal to or less than your PSI score on two dice. If you succeed, turn to **3**. If you fail, turn to **245**.

254

You reach up and grasp the hilt of the sword. The golden strand snaps as you tug it. You hold the sword out and test its balance. It is a fine, though unremarkable, weapon. Note it on your Character Sheet and continue by turning to **113**.

255

You step past the lion's body. As you do so, you notice that it had a large thorn stuck right through its paw. Just as well you killed it – it was probably in a vile temper and might have attacked someone. Turn to **24**.

256

You return to The Four Leaf Clover inn. There are a couple of labourers enjoying flagons of ale. Will you attempt to steal the horse brass in the shape of a clover leaf that hangs over the bar (turn to **106**), or will you adopt a more straightforward approach and ask the innkeeper (turn to **294**)?

257

Slank advances on you with a panther's grace, his robes fluttering in the breeze. There is a cold, damp, earthy smell like a waiting grave. You see that the talons of his right hand are almost a cubit long; they sparkle like crystal and are obviously razor-sharp.

SLANK   VIGOUR 24

Roll two dice:
score 2 to 8   You are struck; lose 3 VIGOUR
score 9 to12   The demon loses 3 VIGOUR

If you manage to defeat him, turn to **137**.

258

There is no one there – just two empty boots standing in an alcove. You step back in surprise, then whirl around as a snarl of annoyance warns you that you are about to be attacked. A mad Dwarf is running towards you on stockinged feet, furious that you were not taken in by his ploy. Turn to **81** for the fight, but you must subtract 2 from the dice roll in the first Combat Round only, to represent his advantage of surprise.

259

Your fingers have just closed around the brass when you hear a shout from behind: 'Hey, Bruno, y've got a thief in yer bar!' You turn to find that several heavyset men are already closing in on you clutching cudgels and broken bottles. You pocket the brass and draw your sword grimly.

BRUNO the Innkeeper	VIGOUR 9
OLAF the Blacksmith	VIGOUR 12
TORRICK the Ruffian	VIGOUR 9
JARED the Tailor	VIGOUR 6

Roll two dice:

score 2   You are hit four times; lose 12 VIGOUR

score 3   You are hit three times; lose 9 VIGOUR

score 4 to 5   You are hit twice; lose 6 VIGOUR

| score 6 to 7 | You are hit once; lose 3 VIGOUR |
| score 8 to 12 | One of them (you decide which) loses 3 VIGOUR |

You cannot get to the door because they are blocking your way. If you slay one, turn to **161** (remember to note down the VIGOUR scores of the others first).

260

Unfortunately, you cannot find any tracks to support your theory. With a shrug you turn away from the idol and return to the path to head west, towards the hills. Turn to **301**.

261

You point out an unsightly dent in his breastplate and offer to rush with it to the armourer so that it can be repaired before the joust begins. He thanks you effusively and quickly removes the armour, giving it to you along with three Gold Pieces for your trouble. Unfortunately, the armourer's tent is nearby and so you have no opportunity to steal a fragment as you carry his breastplate over. Once inside the tent, you hand the breastplate to the armourer. You watch him hammering the dent out and realize you are going to have to bribe him. Decide how much you will offer and then turn to **49**.

262

A bank of mist rolls in front of you. You walk forward through the mist but cannot find the crystal ball anywhere. Somewhat perplexed, you decide to return to the path and continue on. Turn to **115**.

263

You enquire whether she has any lucky heather to sell you. As she goes to the back of the caravan to get some, you scoop up the crystal ball and back away to the door. But as you fumble with the drapes she turns, and you hear her call on the spirits of the departed to curse you. Try to roll equal to or less than your *current* PSI on two dice. If you succeed, turn to **21**. If you fail, turn to **119**.

264

You step through the doorway and advance along a dank passage. Peering through an archway to your right, you espy the scarlet and gold outlines of a bizarre demonic face hanging in the blackness before you. A luminous mask on the far wall of the chamber, perhaps? You thrust your lantern forward, but it does little to pierce the thick shadows. If you wish to go through the archway, turn to **298**. If you would rather continue along the passage, turn to **251**.

(illustration on following page)

Curse the luck! Your knife breaks. If you did not have a sword then you are now without any weapon at all, and in future combats you will inflict only 2-point wounds on your opponent instead of the usual 3 points. If you do have a sword, you are certainly not going to risk breaking *its* blade on the ice. You decide to leave the damned mask where it is and take a look through the archway. Turn to **288**.

Your ring emits a blinding pulse of light, but this has no effect whatsoever on the creature. It strikes you with a watery fist as you fumble for your weapon – lose 3 VIGOUR points from this blow, then turn to **33**.

You drop your remaining supply of the Salve into the ravenous 'hole', which is unimpressed by the substance's foul taste and hurriedly spits you out into the open air. The hailstorm has now passed. Turn to **69**.

You panic and run for the archway, but your feet slip on the ice and you scramble frantically on all fours. Roll six dice, attempting to score equal to or less than your *current* VIGOUR. If you succeed, turn to **29**. If you fail, turn to **218**.

269

You return to the Faze mansion, now with the four of the six items you need for your quest. Only the saint's ashes and the hair of a nun remain to be found – but Jasper suggests that since the town is not an especially holy place, you may have more luck obtaining the last two items on your way to the Castle of Lost Souls.

You spend a couple of days studying maps and travellers' accounts, planning your route to the demon's keep. (If you are wounded, regain 2 VIGOUR points for the rest.) The evening before you are due to set out, you gaze from the library windows towards the setting sun. In that direction lies the Castle – but in this world, or in the next? You yawn and close the compendium of charts you have been studying. Whatever awesome perils await you, there is little to be gained from dwelling upon them now. Turn to **47**.

270

You are just putting the brass into your pocket when someone yells: 'Put that back, you lightfing-ered scum!' There is a mighty crash. You whirl, drawing your sword. A huge man is advancing on you with a broken bottle in one hand and the leg of a stool in the other. As you edge away, the innkeeper comes out from behind the bar clutching a meat cleaver. He blocks your retreat and you must fight them both.

BRUNO the Innkeeper   VIGOUR 9
ANVIL the Wrestler   VIGOUR 15

Roll two dice:

score 2 to 3   You are struck twice; lose 6 VIGOUR

score 4 to 5   You are struck once; lose 3 VIGOUR

score 6 to 12   One of your enemies (you choose which) loses 3 VIGOUR

If you defeat one of them, turn to **54**.

271

Wearily you trudge up to another crossroads. You are starting to think you have been going around in circles when you see the force-field walls dissolving like fragments of dream. In a rush of cold air you are lifted upwards to a vast hall of mirrors. As an instant of disorientation passes, you look down to find a solid floor beneath your feet. Behind you, the door through which you passed earlier stands open. Shaking your head in puzzlement, you wonder whether you were truly caught in a maze at all – perhaps it was an illusion spell with which Slank hoped to ensnare your mind. Seeing an archway at the end of the hall, you hurry towards it and pass on into the next room. Turn to **299**.

272

The doors do not look any different when you examine them through the gypsy's crystal ball. Turn back to **147** and think again.

273

Now that you possess the crystal ball, the teardrop and the four leaf clover, all you need is a fragment of a chivalrous knight's armour. Will you:

Go to the joust being held tomorrow?	Turn to **36**
Go to see Hrothgar, a scholar who is renowned for his private collection of arms and armour?	Turn to **152**

274

You hastily nock an arrow on to your bow and take aim at the retreating Chonchon leader. To hit it, you must roll 3 or higher on one die. You have time for but one shot before it is out of range. If you hit, turn to **78**. If you miss, turn to **222**.

275

'Excellent. After killing Slank you must scatter the ashes over his body. Now, I wish you good luck.' You shake hands before taking your leave of him and continuing along the corridor. Behind you, you hear him pushing the library furniture back against the door. Turn to **134**.

276

You descend a flight of stairs into what seems to be a pillared ballroom with a floor of polished white marble. There is a shadowed archway across on the other side of the room. However, as you walk warily towards this, you make a startling discovery – the floor underfoot is not marble at all, but solid ice. Several inches below you, frozen in the ice, you can see a bizarre demonic mask. As you peer down at this you suddenly realize how cold the room is getting. Your hands are turning blue and your teeth chatter uncontrollably. Do you have a bearskin rug? If so, turn to **18**. If not, turn to **268**.

(illustration on following page)

277

You find a twisting flight of steps leading up out of the dungeon. To your immense relief, the door at the top is not locked and you emerge into the candlelit entrance hall. You decide to try the stairs – turn to **103**.

278

They tell you that there is an old hermit outside the town who might well have such an item, as he collects curios and odd artifacts. They are prepared to take you to his hut, but you will have to pay them five Gold Pieces for their trouble. You could go with them straight away (turn to **286**), or first ask if they know where you could find a four leaf clover (turn to **42**). If you will not pay their price, you could walk over to the bar and either chat to the innkeeper (turn to **227**) or pilfer the horse brass you noticed earlier (turn to **190**).

279

You pass along a winding tunnel and enter a vaulted room lit with a sombre green radiance. A dark silhouette takes form in front of you. A tall, majestic woman. She is – magnificent. You stand in awe. A watery green hue dissolves from the room as she lifts the veil covering her face and you stare directly into the unfiltered light of her eyes. They shine like polished jade. You try to turn away but you cannot break her mesmerizing gaze.

Mournful voices seem to echo in your head, greeting you – the voices of a hundred stony victims entrapped by the Gorgon to become her companions and lovers. They stand in shadowed alcoves all about. Your world is with theirs now. Share silence . . .

280

You hurl your sword away and the Marshons scurry after it. They seize the gleaming object and carry it off. As they recede into the night you can hear their shrill, bubbly voices disputing ownership of this new prize. You are safe, but from now on you will have to use a dagger instead of a sword in combat, so all your Combat Rolls must be reduced by 1. For example, you would count Dice Roll of 7 in Combat as though it were a 6. Turn to **66**.

281

You ransack his home in search of treasure he may have looted from travellers less wary or skilled than yourself. You find a magic Ring of Light, five Gold Pieces and a potion in a blue bottle. If you drink the potion, either now or later in the adventure, turn to **95** to find out what it does. You may drink it at any time except during a combat; remember to note the paragraph number you are at first, because **95** will not redirect you to that entry.

Under the floorboards you are revolted to discover human bones from more than thirty bodies, neatly arranged in boxes with notes on the quality of each person's conversation and flavour. You pass the rest of the night in a fitful sleep full of harrowing nightmares and depart before the sun is up, eager to be away from this dreadful place. Turn to **132**.

282

Smiling viciously, Slank steps from the alcove and stands before you, huge and awesome and *casting no shadow*. You hear the rumble of the approaching storm, drowned out by Slank's laughter. His surcoat and boots and vambraces are as black as the night and trimmed with silver; his pale skin has a translucent gleam. At first glance the face might almost be considered handsome – but then you see the clouded, sightless right eye, the face around it scarred and mutilated by terrible burns. The good eye shines with an awful, corrupt light and the expression twisting those fine features is one of utter and inhuman evil.

Slank holds a lacquered mask in his left hand, and he brings this up now to cover his face. The mask has a quartz lens which shields his good eye, so even if you have the teardrop you cannot use it. Neither is there time to draw your bow – you must fight him. Turn to **257**.

283

The fourth Chonchon, which has been hovering over you watching the fight, now starts to beat its ears furiously and fly off across the marsh. If you defeat any remaining Chonchons within two Combat Rounds (refer back to **84** if you can't remember their VIGOUR scores) you may try to bring down the escaping leader with an arrow – turn to **274**.

If the fight goes on longer than two Combat Rounds then the leader is out of bowshot. If you kill the remaining Chonchons after that, turn to **222**.

284

You walk along a short corridor and come to a low door. If you want to go through this door, turn to **199**. If you want to turn back and go the other way, turn to **27**.

285

The man, whose name is Garl, feeds you with a delicious and nourishing stew. The wine he has to offer is also excellent – nothing like the rough homebrew you were expecting. Garl is clearly even more drunk than you thought. He sits in his armchair watching you eat, taking great gulps from his mug and saying things such as 'You are an adventurer who has performed deeds of merit while I am but a hermit with a dubious past. Yet when we belch, where then is the difference between us?' Finally, noticing you stifle a yawn, he shows you to your room. You may go to sleep (turn to 35) or sit up and keep watch (turn to 188).

286

They lead you into the woods outside the town, along a pathway that can have seen little use over the past few years. You are beginning to get suspicious. You turn to see one of them drawing his sword as he creeps up on you! He shouts to the others, and all three rush in to the attack.

First ADVENTURER	VIGOUR 12
Second ADVENTURER	VIGOUR 9
Third ADVENTURER	VIGOUR 9

Roll two dice:

score 2 to 3	You are hit three times – lose 9 VIGOUR
score 4 to 5	You are hit twice – lose 6 VIGOUR
score 6 to 7	You are hit once – lose 3 VIGOUR
score 8 to 12	One of them (you choose which) loses 3 VIGOUR

Once you have defeated one, make sure you have recorded the remaining VIGOUR scores of the other two and then turn to **86**.

287

You return to The Four Leaf Clover inn. The gypsies are still here. They have had quite a lot to drink, and one of them is now playing a jig on his fiddle. If you wish to join them at their table, turn to **56**. If you go over and talk to the innkeeper, turn to **227**. The clover-leaf horse brass still hangs enticingly above the bar; if you wish to try and steal it, turn to **190**.

288

You are at the foot of a rough stone stairway that winds up around the walls of a narrow, circular tower. Staring into the gloom, you discern a crimson glow far above. You climb up and up – hundreds of feet, it seems. At last you reach the top of the tower. There is only one door off the landing – a heavy iron portal with a glowing, gloating red face inscribed into it. It swings back as you step towards it, and you pass through into what must be the topmost chamber of the tower. The wind shrieks through the open windows. Outside you can see massive, ponderous storm clouds against the starless night sky. There is a curtained alcove on the other side of the chamber. As you cross over to it, a sibilant voice seems to

speak from within you, extolling the virtues of an eternity in service to the demon. Roll two dice. If you score less than or equal to your PSI score, turn to **45**. If the dice roll exceeds your PSI score, turn to **206**.

289

The ancient crown fits comfortably on your brow. As you lower your hands, you fancy you hear a spectral whispering. It comes closer, and faint images begin to form around you. Hundreds of pallid figures throng the crypt, reaching to you in supplication. You see them only mistily, as though through a veil of tears, but their voices are clearer now: 'Return to us, majesty. How we have longed to have you with us again . . .'

A tiny thrill of dread gives way to a ghastly calm. You find yourself clambering into the empty sarcophagus. An unseen force must be lifting the lid, for you are soon enclosed in utter darkness. A sweet silence reigns. Peacefully, you wait to join your subjects in death.

290

As you step towards the fireplace, the rug comes to life and rises up, challenging you with an eerie hissing growl.

BEARSKIN RUG   VIGOUR 12

Roll two dice:
score 2 to 5   You are hit; lose 3 VIGOUR
score 6 to 12   The Rug loses 3 VIGOUR

If you FLEE past it to the doors, turn to **276**. If
you defeat it, turn to **211**.

291

Four of them see you coming and leave their
companions to slaughter the guard while they deal
with you. You adopt a watchful stance as they
surround you; these four will be difficult to beat.

EMAJ DOGBREATH	VIGOUR 9
IPCOLL the Sour	VIGOUR 9
UKNOR the Barbarian	VIGOUR 12
BOSO HEADCUT	VIGOUR 9

Roll two dice:

score 2	You are hit four times – lose 12 VIGOUR
score 3 to 4	You are hit three times – lose 9 VIGOUR
score 5 to 6	You are hit twice – lose 6 VIGOUR
score 7 to 8	You are hit once – lose 3 VIGOUR
score 9 to 12	One of the robbers (you choose) loses 3 VIGOUR

you kill one, turn to **28**. If you decide to FLEE,
you run the risk of losing 12 VIGOUR points (all

four will hit you if you fail the AGILITY roll) – turn to **219**.

292

He reaches into a pouch at his belt and produces a number of wicked-looking devices. 'Pilliwinks is a game played with the fingers,' he explains as he fixes the thumbscrews on to you. Paralysing pain shoots up your arms. Through waves of agony you see the figure before you dissolve and alter – he is no longer an old man, but a tall figure clad in black robes.

'A generous soul is a lost soul,' says Slank with a demonic smile. 'Allow me to welcome you as my castle's latest guest.'

Your adventure has ended, but the torment is just beginning . . .

293

As Slank flails about blindly, you raise your bow and shoot the specially prepared arrow straight into his evil heart. He falls dead at your feet. Turn to **137**.

294

The innkeeper tells you that there are sometimes four leaf clovers to be found in the beer garden behind the inn. 'Why d'ye think it's called The Four Leaf Clover?' he laughs. You go out to the beer garden. A sleek cat is lazing in the sun. It is black, except for a patch of white fur around one eye. You bend down to stroke it, and as you do your gaze falls upon a four leaf clover by its paw. Delighted, you pluck the clover (note it down on your Character Sheet) and leave the inn, ignoring the astonished stares of the innkeeper and his patrons. Turn to **273**.

295

You realize that Garl is not a human being at all, but a cold-hearted Ogre, hungry for your flesh!

OGRE   VIGOUR 15

Roll two dice:
score 2 to 6   You are hit; lose 4 VIGOUR
score 7 to 12   The Ogre loses 3 VIGOUR

Note that Garl's blows inflict more damage than usual, because of his fearsome strength. If you beat him, turn to **281**.

You spot a niche in the ridge and scramble up the slope to it. The ledge is quite wide, and you are able comfortably to stretch out on it. It is a good place to spend a night: wolves and the like will be unable to reach you. After a meal of bread and cheese washed down with some excellent brandy from Jasper's cellar, you settle down to a relaxing sleep. You awaken early. If you have any wounds, recover 1 VIGOUR point for your rest. You gather your belongings and continue onwards. Turn to **132**.

If you have any magical potions you have time to drink one or more of them now before engaging the robbers in combat. Decide, and then turn to **291**.

Holding your lantern aloft and treading warily in the deep darkness, you approach the glinting lines of the demon-mask. A sob of terrified breath catches in your throat as you hear an ominous hiss – you know at once that you are not looking at a mask but at the head of a Giant Cobra! It turns towards you, and its scales glisten like polished jet in your lamplight. As it rears up and slithers across the flagstones, you see its slender tongue dart in and out like a flickering red flame. Its jaws are wet with lethal venom, and you quickly prepare to defend yourself from its attack.

GIANT COBRA   VIGOUR 12

Roll two dice:
score 2   Turn to **31**
score 3 to 5   You are hit; lose 3 VIGOUR
score 6 to 12   The Cobra loses 3 VIGOUR

If you FLEE back to the passage and hurry on, turn to **251**. If you kill the Giant Cobra, turn to **123**.

299

Beyond the arch lies a long, oak-panelled room through which a chilling draught blows. There is a pit covered by a heavy grating in the floor, and beside it rests a coil of rope. If you wish to take a closer look at the pit, turn to **156**. If you walk across the room and leave via the corridor at the far end, turn to **2**.

300

You open the door into what seems to be a kitchen. It is full of smoke and steam and is almost unbearably hot. Looking around you, you see a cauldron bubbling over the roaring fire and a small doorway to one side that presumably leads to the larder. Directly across the kitchen from where you

entered is a copper-bound door stamped with odd runic designs. You can look in the larder (turn to **63**), inspect the contents of the cauldron (turn to **183**) or go through to the next room, (turn to **240**).

301

You trudge on for many miles. It is late in the afternoon and the sun is dipping towards the rolling Mungo Hills ahead of you. You are trying to estimate whether you will be into the hills by nightfall when you see a skirmish of some kind on the road ahead. Cautiously you advance until you can discern the details. A small robber band has attacked a group of wayfarers. Two guards lie dead in the dust and a third is battling against hopeless odds to prevent the robbers from getting to the coach he was accompanying. You see an old man cowering beside the coach. Will you:

Rush to help the guard?	Turn to **297**
Pick off the robbers with your bow?	Turn to **198**
Avoid getting involved?	Turn to **189**

302

As soon as he has the rope, he grins and gives it a sharp tug. You utter a short cry of alarm as you lose your balance and fall into the pit. Demonic laughter reverberates around you as you fall.

Landing knocks all the air from your lungs, and it is a few moments before you are able to stand. You are alone in the dark pit. A scraping of metal makes you look up. The one-eyed man, now in the room above, is sliding the grating back across. It fits into place with a dreadful clang.

'Welcome,' says Slank, 'to the Castle of Lost Souls.'

303

The little girl's teardrop is like an acid to Slank. He screams in rage and pain and clutches at his eye. Did Luther Faze explain to you the purpose of the armour fragment and the nun's hair? If so, turn to **293**. If not, turn to **172**.

304

You step over the coils of the dead serpent and begin a search of the room. The darkness here seems unnaturally thick; finally you decide to leave your lantern by the arch and resort to feeling your way around the walls. You discover no other exits, but you do come across a heavy chest which you presume the cobra was set here to guard. If you wish to open the chest, turn to **214**. If you would rather first pull it out into the passage, where you have more light, turn to **186**.

305

You gulp back the magic potion. For the duration of your fight with the Undine, you add 1 to the dice roll each Combat Round. Turn to **33**.

306

You soon tire of the captain's monomaniacal ranting about law and retribution. You excuse yourself and go off in search of the Mother Superior. She is an altogether more agreeable person, and when you ask her if she could supply you with a nun's hair she laughs merrily. 'Norwena has just had her head shaved to join our Order,' she says. She glides away and soon returns with a long black strand of hair. You put this in your backpack as she shows you to the door. 'You are always welcome here,' she tells you. You turn at the gate to wave to her, and see the captain watching you like a mad hawk from an upper window. With an uneasy shiver, you hurry westwards. Turn to **252**.

307

You have no trouble in breaking the rusty manacles from his wrists. 'What a generous soul you are!' he exclaims, favouring you with a rather peculiar smile. 'How about a game of pilliwinks?' Will you accept his offer (turn to **292**), or decline to play (turn to **150**)?

You catch a furtive flurry of movement out of the corner of your eye. Unless it is your imagination, there is someone hiding behind one of the curtains. You strain your ears and detect a soft rustle of fabric, a muffled intake of breath. Silently you unsheathe your blade and step nearer. Two boots protrude from under the drape. Whoever is waiting there, he seems unaware that you have noticed him. Will you:

Strike at him through the curtain?	Turn to **26**
Throw the curtain aside to see who he is?	Turn to **258**
Run to the door at the end of the gallery?	Turn to **38**

From an upper window you watch the exodus of the thousands of souls Slank had kept imprisoned here, some of them for aeons. They file from the castle and out across the swamps, where they fade from your mortal sight as they pass into the afterlife. You scan the milling throng for Luther Faze and finally catch sight of him – capering merrily, he dances away from the castle towards whatever fate the afterlife reserves for merchants . . .

At last you are alone in the castle. You descend through the empty halls and stride away across the marshes. You do not look back until you reach the Mungo Hills, and by then there is no sign of the castle.

As you make your way back towards the town, you find that seers and wizards have already learned of your success. Balladeers roam the villages singing epic songs which tell of the archfiend's destruction and which refer to you as Demonslayer, Knight of Souls, and several other flattering titles.

Jasper and his brothers have invited the whole town to an alfresco party in your honour. You are carried shoulder-high through the streets to the main square, where Jasper delivers a long speech and then presents you with a chest containing a king's ransom in gold, silver and precious jewels! Now that you are rich, you look forward to enjoying your new wealth in the peace and quiet you have earned.